We're All Connected

By: IDA W. BYTHER-SMITH

McClure Publishing, Inc.
Oak Lawn, Illinois

Cover design by Barron Steward (www.barronsteward.com)
Author Photograph by Keith Claunch (www.keithclaunch.com)
Interior Layout by Kathy McClure (www.mcclurepublishing.com)
Edited by Beatrice Daniel
Final Edits by Patrice Dean

To order additional copies, please contact.
McClure Publishing, Inc.
www.mcclurepublishing.com
800.659.4908
mcclurepublishing@msn.com

DEDICATION

This book is dedicated to my late mother, Josephine Robinson Wilson, who always said it's never too late. My children who names are James, Melissa, Lavinia, and Branden. To Rena Winfield, my goddaughter, that wouldn't let me procrastinate which is something I am very good at. Kathy McClure who just walked into my life, and said, "the next one will do better" Patrice Dean, Annie Smith, Karen Ford, and many more of my best friends.

ACKNOWLEDGEMENTS

James E. Byther Son

Artis & Melissa A. Haywood son-in-law and daughter

Branden S. Smith daughter

Lavinia Monique Henderson daughter

Patrice Dean & Annie Smith my best friends

Jennifer Thomas good friend

Members of Christ Outreach C O G I C

New Life Covenant of Oakwood

And all of my family who stands by me through thick and thin.

I just thank GOD for the people He blessed around me.

REVIEWS

Those of you that have heard of Ida W. Byther-Smith might be under the impression that this book is about HIV/AIDS. I assure you this is a love story, and it is full of romance and ups and downs of life. Anything Ida chooses to write, she gives it her all.

Ida's first book, "A Woman Story Over Coming the Shame of HIV" was centered more on her personal story and stories of two other women, but We're All Connected is fiction with a little truth. Either way, you will feel the heart of this woman.

Ida came bringing life to you from a man, woman, boy and girls point of view and make you feel the love, the pain, the good, the bad and the ugly side of life.

Ida pulls no punches when it comes to drama, sex, love or hate. She keeps it real.

Her next book: "Wild Woman Blues," will be in stores around Christmas. Hold onto your hats it's real. Love, Patrice Dean

Ida brings you into her world when you start reading her stories. A.A. Rawls

Ida writes with love, feeling, and most of all understanding. Yaa Simpson

---

Ida's intentions are to keep the reader curious about what is going to happen next. GRACE MAGAZINE

Ida's stories are very informative in language that is down-to-earth and easy to understand. Her material is always real and understanding. J.D. Hawkins

PROLOGUE

Not many women can capture the words of a man and make you feel his joy, pain, love; and the growth behind his struggles with life. (The GOOD, the BAD, and THE UGLY) You will find Ms. Byther-Smith keeps it real. Ms. Byther-Smith lives in Chicago while running her own company. She has lived 20 years with HIV; 7 with AIDS. After almost dying, she started writing which is something she loves, but was afraid to do until now. You will not hear her feeling sorry for herself. She puts it best "I did not learn how to live until I almost died." Thank GOD for AIDS!!!!!

Ida W. Byther-Smith

My name is Willie James Bradshaw Jr. I guess mama and my old man couldn't come up with anything better. This probably would have been my name even if I had been a girl. Being the first born my name probably would have been Willie Mae Bradshaw or Willie Jane Bradshaw as long as I was named after him. All my life I have borne the burden of carrying his name. Sometimes I wish I was a woman just so I could get married and take on a different last name. Being the oldest of ten I was determined to do something with my life. I just didn't have a plan to put into action. There were two things I was sure about:

❖ I wouldn't get anybody's daughter pregnant and not take care of the child.

❖ Any woman I said, "I do" to would be made happy at all times.

If things didn't turn out the way I wanted them to, it wouldn't be because I didn't give my best effort to make it work. Looking at my old man I knew I would do without a woman before I put one through the hell my mother went through. She worked two jobs and worked a paper route on Sunday. My old man would lie in bed until 10:00 a.m. and then get up and ask, what's to eat. (He wouldn't hit a snake if it was on his foot until he got a new woman and wanted to impress her).

By 5:00 a.m. my mother would be in the field running the tractor while he would get up, go out on the porch, and wave her in to fix him a meal. Can you believe it? He was fresh from a good night's rest and could have fixed his own meal. She would come in to fix him breakfast. Often I would be back in school, which was something I loved. My best subject was science. My dream was to be the first colored man in space. That dream was crushed the day I told my teacher, Mrs. White, that I wanted to be like John Glenn, the astronaut. With the look on her face, you would have thought I had put my hand up her dress. She asked all the children what their goals in life were. Everyone wanted to be a teacher, nurse, or entertainer. I wanted to be the first colored man in space. That's what they use to call us in the sixties.

"James. James Bradshaw. What would you like to be when you grow up?"

"An astronaut," I replied.

She stood up so fast that her chair tilted over behind her. She walked over to my desk. "Boy, are you crazy? There are no colored men in space, nor are there any colored astronauts."

I felt as if someone had poured ice water all over my body. The only thing that kept going through my mind over and over was what she said. 'There are no colored astronauts in space. There are no colored astronauts in space." I could hear the rest of the class laughing at me. I was glad this class was ending and I would be going to lunch. After class I was feeling sick and I could hardly catch my breath. Instead of going to lunch I sat on the school steps. I am not sure just how long I sat there but I heard Mr. Grammar's voice over the intercom. He was the principal of our school.

"Willie Bradshaw please report to the principal's office immediately. Attention all teachers if you have Willie Bradshaw in your class please send him to the principal's office immediately."

I hurried to the principal's office where my father was waiting. I think this was one of the few times I was happy to see my old man. Mrs. White had called him to the school for a conference with the principal but I didn't know why. I knew he was there to take me home from the tone of the message over the intercom. Any other time I would have been upset but not today. After we left the school grounds, I asked him about the conference and being an astronaut.

"Boy you continuously go on about this crazy notion of someday going to the moon. This is 1962. There is no such thing as a colored man going to the moon. Of course, the only way it would be possible is if the white man and all their descendents passed away. Your future is in learning how to repair cars so you can make some real money with me," he said.

I dropped the subject because I knew that with my father having only a sixth grade education he really believed that he was right. As usual, we wound up cutting grass and working to fix a neighbor's broken down old car. By the time evening came I was starving and dog-tired. I probably would have been out half the night if Mom hadn't called us to say dinner was ready. WJ had left well over an hour earlier, which was his normal ritual. He would get me started working on a car and split. As soon as I got into the house mom asked, "Where is your Daddy?"

"I don't know. He left a little while ago."

"James, don't cover for him. I know he left around 5:30 p.m. I saw him drive off as I was coming in." I wasn't covering up for him. I just didn't want to hurt Mom's feelings and I didn't want to lie either.

"Mom, I really wasn't watching the time and besides I was under the car." Smiling I walked over to the table to eat dinner. "Mom, I want to be an astronaut when I grow up." I just blurted it right out because I wanted to see what her response would be.

She looked at me and asked, "Are you sure? The way you said it I am not convinced that you have given this a lot of thought." I told her what my teacher said earlier in class and how Daddy reacted after telling him after school. She came over and put her arms around me and gave me a hug. "James, I am very proud of you. Go for it if that's what you really want to do. Give it all that you have. Don't let anyone discourage you from realizing your dream. Without dreams we have nothing with which to lay a foundation for our future. You remember one thing and that is nothing beats a fail but a try. Start right now by getting your education. Don't let anyone put an obstacle in your way. You have a lot going for you right now." After talking to Mom I was feeling much better.

Because I had been taken out of class early, I didn't have my assignment for the next day. I knew a girl named Leann who was in my same grade. I knew she would give it to me because not only was she smart, but I believed she liked me as well (she made that very clear). She was always trying to get me to come to her house. She didn't live very far, but I would always find an excuse to avoid going over there. I was always busy trying to balance helping my parents with my siblings, schoolwork, and working on cars with my dad so that I had no time? My father's number one pastime was either working on his car or trying to keep someone else's running. He was making my life unbearable with that, and kicking my mother around (but not necessarily in that order). I walked over to Leann's house, got the homework assignment, and ran out of there quickly.

After I turned 14, I made it very clear that he could no longer hit on my mother anymore. Mom made it perfectly clear that all of us had to respect him at all times. She would always say that he might not be all that nice but he's still your father. I hated when she put it that way.

We all knew the only reason why he married Mom was because she didn't open her legs to him before saying "I do." I sometimes wish she had just slept with him and gotten it over with. Maybe it would have been just the two of us because the minute they got married Mom was pregnant with me. Ten months later I was born. My worst fear, just from watching my mother, was getting married and missing out on life.

When Leann would invite me to her house I would turn down the invitation even if I weren't doing anything. I would always give her some story that she often took to be true. It was clear that she always had more on her mind than books. Leann was a year older than me and built like a brick shit house with each brick laid by a professional. The only problem was when I looked at her mother I always thought twice about being over there. My Uncle Mark said if you wanted to know what a girl would look like after she turned 40 just take a look at her mother. My fear was she was going to look just like her mother when she got older. Leann's mother looked like death riding a soda cracker to a funeral. I couldn't get a hard on with her if I kept it in the freezer all night.

My mother had ten kids, and her stomach and waistline were still flat as a board. Guys were always commenting about how fine my sisters would be when they got older (45 was considered over the hill in my family).

My mother and I were very close but I just couldn't understand why she constantly put up with WJ. Mama was mixed with Black and Indian. She could get any man she wanted. Daddy had a little of everything in him. We called his family Hines 57 because of all the nationalities that run through their family lines. I have this cousin named Beverly that would follow me around when we went to visit them. The girl looked white and had green eyes as well as long straight hair. She got her looks from her father who had the same features. My Aunt Mary, Beverly's grandmother was set up for $50 by her own sister. This white farmer saw her and had to have her. She said no way. He paid Aunt Mary's sister, Aunt Lily, to get her out of the house by telling her she had to use the outhouse, which was, located a distance from the house. When they got there, Butch as they called him, was waiting in the trees. He took Aunt Mary by gunpoint. Aunt Lily walked back toward the house pretending she heard nothing. After Butch was done with Aunt Mary, she was too scared to say anything. This had taken place back in the 1920's. There was nothing that could be done by the time Aunt Mary discovered that she was pregnant.

It turns out that everyone in the family is mixed with something. WJ himself was 6'2" in height, weighed 185 lbs., had smoky dark skin and had thick curly hair. The man was not short stopping when it came to physical appearance but still my mother deserved better.

My mother was another story. Mama stood at 5'11", 180 lbs., and had an hourglass figure. Her only shortfall was she didn't have a big chest. After 10 children and breast-feeding you would have to give up something. To top it off, my mother had natural red hair, which was unusual for a black person. She is the reason that I have inherited this same red hair. For a long time I hated it, but that changed over time. My siblings have WJ's hair and eyes. I was the only black kid I knew who had red hair that wasn't course like my father's. I was definitely my mama's kid. As a matter of fact I think that's what some of the fights between my parents were all about-whether I was his child or not. I heard some wise tail about mama's baby; daddy's maybe, but there was no doubt that I was my father's child because my mother was faithful to him. I knew WJ was my father and if I let myself, I could probably be just as ruthless as he was. I work very hard not to be like his side of the family. Their view on morals was different from my mother's side of the family. His family had no problems with dating or marrying into the family. His cousins and aunts were always trying to hit on me. I would talk to my mother about it but WJ would never believe his precious relatives could do no wrong and stoop that low.

COMPARING FAMILIES

There was competition between the Bradshaw and the Danco's. My mother's maiden name was Danco before she married my no good father. My mother's family married some of the men that the Bradshaw women had slept with. Terry, Mississippi was a very small town about 25 miles out of Jackson. It wasn't unusual to cross family lines. The controversy between the families never really died down; it just wasn't made public knowledge. We never spent much time with the Danco's because of the quiet feud that was going on. I can only remember spending one week with my mother's people. I was about 6 or 7 years old. Her family always made a big deal over me. They would comment that I looked just like their side of the family. Little did they know that every time they said something like that, WJ would go berserk when we got home? He already had constant doubt that I was his child. I was tired of sitting up nights to make sure my father wouldn't get physical with my mother. The first time it happened I was about 10 years old. It happened after a visit to Grandma Danco. I woke up to discover he had a knife to her neck. The rage in me wanted to kill him, especially when I thought about how scared my mother must have been. I stalled by pretending I wanted some water and needed to use the bathroom. We had a fireplace, so I stalled even longer by using the poker iron to move the logs around to keep the fire going in the front room. We were all sleeping in the front room due to not having heat anyplace else in the house because the gas was off. They were all asleep on the floor with the exception of me. I was up and very much alert. I could always tell when something was wrong with Mom. My mother looked at me upon seeing me standing at the couch. I don't even remember how I got there. She knew exactly what was on my mind.

"James honey you better go back to sleep because you have school tomorrow. You don't want to fall asleep in class."

It was amazing how she would concern herself more with WJ than herself. She knew at that moment that

I wanted to bust his skull wide open and think nothing of it. I could see and hear the fear in her voice. I couldn't understand why she had a knife at her throat and was trying to send me back to bed. I returned to bed but I didn't get much sleep. I was up at the crack of dawn looking for any signs that he had put one scar on my mother. She was okay but she was more tired than usual. She gave me that look that said please don't ask me any questions.

I left for school with two friends, Buddy and Larry, who were better known as Dirty Red. Red lived up to his name. I often wondered how often did this guy take a bath or change clothes without someone telling him to do so. Buddy was just the opposite. He was always clean. I couldn't understand why he hung around with either of us. Red on the other hand was very intelligent. He didn't really have to study to pass a test. He'd just look over the lesson quickly and he had the hang of it. On the other hand I had to put forth that extra effort. I knew early on that I wasn't going to get something for nothing.

I worked hard to keep my grades up after Mrs. Taylor got me on the right track. I remember the first day she walked into the classroom. She reminded me of my mother. She was a tall woman, well built and very nice. She wasn't anything like Mrs. White (the teacher who discouraged me from becoming the first black astronaut in space). Not only did she not like me but she didn't like Dirty Red or Buddy either. She always made us sit in the back of the classroom. She stated once that it was a waste of time to try to teach lost souls. She felt that we were not worth her time because we weren't going anywhere to begin with. All the other kids got a real laugh out of her treating us that way. Mrs. Taylor was different. She worked with all the kids. Mrs. Taylor made you feel as if you could do anything you set your mind to. From the day she walked in, I never got any grades under a B+. I was in the fourth grade at the time and had a huge crush on my teacher or whatever you want to call it. It was that motherly attention that she was giving me that stirred my emotions. As the saying goes, every boy wants a girl just like dear old mom. I was no exception to that saying. She had a way with words. Her compliments didn't hurt either, like the time she told me I was going to be a great man someday. Just like mom would say, "Never give up on your dreams and never ever let the little boy in you die." Always keep that smile and your sense of humor. Some women like that in a boy or man. Some just want someone to treat them like their dad did their mother. My sisters didn't want a man like their Dad. I know!

"James, some of the greatest and most powerful men in the world are not muscular. They are smart and that's better." With my size, I wouldn't be considered needing to be protected at 10 years old. I was at 5'6" and still growing. I weighed 120 lbs. I was not fat but tall and muscular for my age. Anyway, I passed that year with flying colors. I won a few trophies and certificates in sports from elementary school. The next year was a shock to my normal routine. We had to move to the country with Granny and Papa. I loved Granny and I was crazy about my step grand father. The thought of having so much distance between us was upsetting. Maybe this situation stemmed from the fact that he and my father just couldn't get along. WJ was only 13 when Mama Dot married Papa Joe. Papa Joe was a hard workingman and my father wasn't. He had no clue about working hard for anything, because since childhood he's had his mother as a safety net. Granny would take Pa's money and give it to my daddy even after he was married to Mom. She would give us money and other things just to make up for the negligence he had subjected us to. By this time, there were seven of us because one died. Seven crumb snatchers were left running around. We were always in the city or out at granny's. This went on for years.

GROWING UP

This was my first year of junior high. I was now 6 feet tall and wearing a size 11 shoe. My mustache was a sign of my maturity into a young man. I wasn't fine but I was what everyone else called handsome. I would say I was a reasonably attractive and intelligent young man. Getting older meant taking on a lot of life's problems on my shoulders. Anyway that's what Papa Joe would say. Sometimes after school when I finished helping him with the chores, we would just sit and talk. He would say, "Willie (he was the only person that got away with calling me that outside of school) you are a hard worker just like your mother. Don't lose that drive. It will benefit you later on in life. Most importantly make sure you get your education. I never got mine but you will need yours to survive in this world. I know your daddy keeps you out of school a lot, but just remember that one day you will be on your own. Even if you don't get your education as a child, make sure you get it as a man. It's something no one can ever take away from you.

I knew Papa Joe had it hard and Granny wasn't helping matters, because she was a diabetic and couldn't work any more. Papa Joe worked hard to support her and she would just try to pick up the slack for my father's shortcomings. People thought she was Ms. Ida's mother instead of WJ's mother the way Mrs. Ida looked after her.

Sometimes Papa Joe and I would sit and talk until the sun went down. The man wasn't educated, but he had a lot of wisdom and knowledge. Our time spent together was enjoyable and it gave me the opportunity to gain some wisdom from him.

FALL 1961

I made the basketball team and was quite good at the game. During the week, I played basketball and while on the weekends I worked odd jobs when I could get away from my parents because they always came to see us on the weekend I wanted to have a little money in my pocket. Sometimes on Friday, WJ would come all the way out to Forest Hill just to pull me out of school to spend the weekend with him working on his car or someone else's free of charge. This is the year that I met Linda.

Just like Leann, Linda was always willing to give me class notes when I was absent from school. We would sometimes eat lunch together whenever I could afford it. When money was tight, I would spend my lunch hour in the gym hanging with the other guys. By that time I hadn't seen Buddy or Dirty Red in almost a year. They still lived in the city. I really didn't have many friends to talk to with the exception of a few guys that were on the team. Since I was riding the bus I had to make sure I was on the last one, which was for the guys that played sports. Playing sports didn't leave much time for socializing or developing relationships.

My first kiss came the week before Christmas. A few of us were standing in the hallway talking about the Vietnam War among other things. Linda Stewart walked up, put her arms around my neck and standing on her tiptoes she planted a kiss right on my lips. It felt so good that I had to put my hand in my pocket because all the guys had an idea what was happening to me. My whole body was reacting to her kiss. I didn't want it to be known that my manhood was rising because I was blessed in that area. I was both shocked and embarrassed. If they knew one kiss could stir up such a reaction, they would no doubt have something to say. Of course it would be something of a derogatory nature about her and I wasn't into that type of conversation.

In my opinion a brother should treat all women the same way they would want other brothers to treat their female family members. My facial expression must have startled her because she gave me an unusual look as if she had done something wrong. I didn't want to hurt her feelings or give the guys something to talk about, so I put my arms around her and smiled. That gave the guys something to think about. That just fed into most of the guy's egos. Everyone had just finished bragging about how much loving they were getting (If they could get it, neither would know what to do with it). We were good at lying because I know the only thing I was getting was smelly underwear from wet dreams, but no one needed to know that. I had to lie because I didn't want the guys to know I was still a virgin at 13½. I had a reputation to live up to. Linda upheld my reputation when she surprised me with that kiss. My mother knew I wasn't doing anything but not WJ. I would never live that down, which was one more thing I was confused about. WJ said that I should "sow my wild oats" before I settle down with one woman, while the girls were told not to do anything. There was a double standard here. How can boys be told to be bad while the girls are told to be good? Where would I get sex from, the air? Also if you got lucky with a girl, she was labeled as a tramp or 'easy' and you would never marry someone like her. But I had made up my mind that if I met a girl who made me feel good and I was happy, I was going to keep her around and not be concerned with what anyone said.

The guys were commenting on how cool and romantic I looked with Linda in my arms. If they had bothered to look any closer they would have discovered my entire body was shaking. I knew Linda felt it too but she said nothing about it. She just kissed me, smiled, and walked away without looking back. The next day I got a call from her.

"James, I want to know if you are free tonight? We are having a surprise party for my brother Neal, and

I want you to come. Please say you will be here. I'll be fun."

I told her I could come but I knew I would first have to clear it with granny. If she were going to church I would have to baby sit. Of course I would never tell Linda that. Arriving home I went straight to granny's room and asked if I could go to the party. She was overjoyed with happiness (can you believe it?). She wanted me to get out and do more social things. Right now my social life revolved around my sister who wouldn't think of going anywhere without me or my other sister even if it were 12:00 p.m. on Sunday. Another double standard. I was allowed to go out socially alone while I had to tag along with my sister every time she went out. There was only a year and a half between Liz and me.

"Yes baby, young men need to get out sometimes." My mother's exact words that were always a part of my thought process. 'James don't do anything to anyone's sister that you wouldn't want done to yours. Remember what goes around comes back around.' I knew I would have killed anyone who mistreated my sisters or brothers.

After taking a bath and combing my hair I was ready to get dressed. Thanks to my uncle I had some cool threads to put on. I went with a tan silk shirt and brown slacks. Although he was a few years my senior I looked real good in his clothes.

I arrived at Linda's house around 7:30 p.m. I was curious when I didn't hear any music playing inside. What kind of party doesn't have music blasting? I knocked on the door. Linda answered looking like a goddess. My approval showed all over my face. My mouth opened but nothing came out. I was nervous and my legs were stiff. She grabbed me by the hand. All I could see was the skirt and blouse she had on. Her clothes fit perfectly in all the right places. Everything Linda had on complimented her looks. Her clothes fit so snuggly that it made her look very enticing. The word was out about her. She had a reputation with most of the guys in sports but overall she was a very nice person. Looking around I was wondering if I was the first to have arrived.

"Where is everybody?" I asked while trying not to show my disappointment and fear. I didn't want to be alone with Linda because I was really afraid of what might happen. I wasn't built of steel nor was I the most honorable guy in school. I wondered why she would go through all this trouble to make it possible for us to be alone.

"Oh James didn't I tell you? This is a party just for you and me." I must have looked as if I was going to run out the door because in her sweetest voice she convinced me to sit down.

"Don't be afraid. I don't want to embarrass you James nor do I want to make you feel uncomfortable. I already know you're 'innocent'."

"Innocent?"

"Yes. A virgin."

"How do you know that? What makes you think that?"

"When we were kissing I could feel the nervousness in your body, but I must admit that you played it off well. I took it as a sign of your inexperience. There are refreshments in the kitchen. Would you like something cold to drink? Maybe a coke or beer?"

"Yes. Thank you but I don't drink alcohol. A coke would be fine." I didn't bother to tell her that half the men in my family were alcoholics. She probably wouldn't have believed me any way. When she went to the kitchen, I looked around and noticed that they had a very nice home. I thought my granny's was nice but it didn't compare to this one. The house had a country air to it that allowed nature to take its course. It was so perfect that it looked like something taken directly out of a fairy tale. The four bedrooms, two baths home sat in the middle of plush green and beautiful land that stretched for miles to come. Inside the house was a feeling of home sweet home. The brown hardwood floors had a fresh shine, which was evidence of constant upkeep. You could almost see your reflection. The house was decorated to reflect a country scene with its expensive wooden furniture freshly finished, china cabinets filled with distinct china pieces and furniture filled with pastel that added to the home's beautiful décor. The smell of fresh flowers was a reminder of just how refreshing it is to live in the country. She returned with two cokes passing one to me.

"Do you want to come up to my room and check out my record collection?" I looked puzzled without responding. "Relax, my family went out and Neal is spending the night at a friend's house." Taking a long swallow of the coke I realized that it taste different from most cokes I've tasted before. "Let's go upstairs." I followed her this time and I was feeling a little more relaxed. Maybe it was the coke that did it. She put on Marvin Gaye's album. I loved Marvin Gaye so it was as if she was reading my mind. The song, *Pride and Joy,* was telling me to dance so we started dancing. I could dance well because my dad was good at it and took the time to teach us the latest dances on Sunday's after church. I drank more coke. This time it was really good so I drank more. The next record was a slow one. Linda put her arms around my neck and started rubbing my back. That was a turn on for me. This kind of touching always made my manhood rise no matter how hard I tried to stay calm. She knew it, which was why she kept doing it. She was reading my body language like a book.

"James would you like more coke or anything?" I really didn't want to let her go because I was feeling really good. At the same time I was nervous and afraid of what might happen next. Stalling for time was the next best move.

"Yes if you don't mind." When she returned with my coke her blouse was open. Her golden brown breasts were revealed. I could see that she had very nice breasts with big round nipples that were hard. As she approached me she gently slid her skirt off. The only attire that remained on her was a pair of red satin panties. I now knew what Uncle Mark meant by getting turned on. At that moment I was about to explode, I was so turned on. I took the coke from her hand and sat it down on the table. My mind was spinning. As I looked at her almost naked body, she was beautiful. The only thing I could think about was being inside of her but I didn't want to show how anxious I was. If we actually go through with this I had some idea as to what to do although I was still a virgin. I had two or three rubbers in my pocket to prevent us from conceiving a child that we both weren't ready for. My Uncle Mark schooled me when he gave me the condoms. He said never get too excited before you put your "rain coat" on which was his term for a condom. Linda came over and sat right next to me. She started rubbing my back and between my legs. Then we started kissing like there was no tomorrow. I unhooked my pants so my manhood could be available for her touch. By this time her blouse was history. Her breasts were so soft and tasted oh so good. I remember Uncle Mark saying to play with them one at a time and if she let you suck them that's even better. This was obviously a turn on for her because she was moaning and groaning and begging me not to stop. I pulled away from her long enough to put on my raincoat because I knew what releasing without a condom meant and what it could cost you. Meanwhile, Linda was lost in passion.

Linda had removed her panties and I removed my pants and anything else that would stand in the way of being close to Linda. We inched closer to the bed where I gently laid beside her. Before I knew it she was on her back and guiding me inside her warm body. It wasn't as tight as I thought it would be for the size of my manhood was about 9". I wanted this moment to last so I had to practice control to avoid climaxing too fast. Uncle Mark had taught me to always control the point at which you climax even if you were intoxicated. Always make sure the woman makes the first sign of completion. If it seems as if you are going to climax first, think about something else. For example, something you didn't like so well, but well enough to keep going until the job was finished. Never ever do anything halfway. Whatever you do, do it to the best of your ability. I was brought back to reality by the touch of Linda's hands. I could feel her fingernails on my back and I could feel her accepting my manhood. I pulled her closer to me. I had never climaxed like this before. Right at our point of climax the sound of our voices filled the air. She made me feel as if we had become one person, one spirit, and one soul. When it was over I was embarrassed about how vocal I was, but I felt as if I could move a mountain. I rolled over beside Linda not sure if she felt as good as I did.

"Just relax, you were great. Are you sure you have never done this before with a girl?"

"I'm sure."

She had a lot of experience for a 15-year-old girl. She pulled the condom off and threw it in the garbage can. Linda had no hang ups about anything. After discarding the condom, she thoroughly cleaned me up. At that moment, I was ready to start again. I was lying there wondering how much of this I was going to share with Uncle Mark. Before I could complete that thought, Linda was kissing me all over. She looked at me with a devious smile on her face. Her hands began to move over my body in slow motion. My emotions begin to stir when I felt her hand caressing my testicles. No books or conversation with Uncle Mark had prepared me for what was happening right now. I felt her mouth on me, wet and soft. I didn't know anything could feel this good. At that moment I jumped up. She might think that I was going to return the favor and I was not quite prepared to do that. I pushed her so hard that she almost hit the floor.

"James, I am sorry I shouldn't have done that. Please don't be upset with me."

"I'm not upset. It's just that I am inexperienced with some things."

"Don't worry. I am not going to ask you to do anything that you are not comfortable with. I just feel comfortable enough with you to try new things knowing that you won't kiss and tell. This is my first time exploring new things as well. I heard some of the girls in the bathroom talking about the things they did behind closed doors. My first thought was it wouldn't hurt to try these things. I am really enjoying you so just relax and let me enjoy myself." I gave her a puzzled look but I wasn't about to object to anything that she was doing when she put it that way. Live and learn I thought.

"Don't think that I didn't enjoy it because I did. You are very good at it but I want this to be a mutual thing." I relaxed on the bed and let her have her way with me. She started licking me all over. As she moved her tongue over my body my emotions began to explode. She moved toward my manhood. This experience with her felt so good that I wanted to explode. My mind said never let her go. She sat there staring at me afterwards for about thirty seconds to see what my reaction was going to be. I took her in my arms and kissed her. I didn't want her to feel that I thought less of her. After all we enjoyed each other and it was mutual. I could feel her relax in my arms. I entered her again without a condom this time and right away I knew I would hate to be required to use a condom in the future. This time I felt I was making love. Her moaning with ecstasy showed me that I could satisfy a woman's sexual desires. I wasn't worried about ever having to satisfy myself after that experience. I could make love all night it felt so good.

After about two hours of exploring each other's body she lay in my arms and slept like a baby. Later on we talked and that's when she told me she had been with one other guy that was older than her, but she refused to tell me his name. She said it was best that I didn't know. She said her experience with him reflected how insensitive he was. After having sex he would get up, put on his clothes, and leave.

"We never talked like this afterward." Linda was a nice girl and I couldn't see why anyone would be so cold to her. I left her house that evening around 11:45 p.m. When I arrived at home Granny was in bed but Papa Joe was still up.

"Papa Joe you didn't have to wait up for me."

"I wasn't waiting up for you son. I couldn't sleep but since you are here now would be good time for us to have a chat." I sat down wondering what this chat was all about. Papa Joe was a wise old man in my mind so I didn't mind listening when he talked. He had been around for a long time. He had experienced a lot of things that I have yet to experience.

"Willie I know you went to a party at the Stewart's house. I've seen that young lady quite often and word is that Bo's son, Don, is involved with her."

"Don? He is 23 years old."

"Yes he is son. Now let me give you a few pointers that someday you will pass on to your children. Every young man should know these things. Let me impart onto you that girls mature a lot faster than boys in almost every way but they are very volatile when it comes down to their emotions especially when they feel the right man has come along. Whatever you do, try to treat all women the same way that you would want men to treat your mother or sisters. Never treat a woman like you see your Daddy treat your Mother. If it were any other woman he would probably be dead. Your mother is one of the best women I've seen come along in a long time. When I was young and inexperienced, I met a girl just like her. I let her slip away and I have regretted it ever since. (I knew my Granny was a good woman but she could be cold and ruthless when necessary). Don't get me wrong I love your Granny with all my heart but there is only one or two times in a life time that you will meet your soul mate whether she's a saint or whore. Either way she could be your soul mate."

"Whore?" I asked with a puzzled look on my face. If this was wisdom then he was stretching the definition.

"Yes, a whore! Don't let anyone tell you that all good women can be found in the church. Not every woman is in the street because she wants to be. For every woman that walks the street some man put her there. Willie please reverts from marrying a woman just because you can't sleep with her first. Never feel that she is someone you just have to have physically. A real man doesn't expect to get everything he wants when he wants it. Sometimes we get in trouble because our wants are greater than our needs.

There's nothing wrong with walking away to save yourself."

"I have just three more things I want you to remember; in case time is not on our side for a while to allow us time to talk:

* If a woman sleeps with you on the first date that doesn't mean she will sleep with everyone she meets on the first date. Don't get me wrong there are some that will. Some women will sleep with a snake if you hold his head. You will learn that with time and experience. I can't teach you everything by talking, which is why we call what we live each day life. You will learn by doing as you live each day.

* If you meet a woman and she has children, remember that she's a package deal. If she doesn't take care of her kids, my best advice to you is to stay away from her. If her kids don't listen to anyone but her stay away from her because they won't respect you. Never agree to feed any child that doesn't respect you as a man.

* Never eat from a table and not put anything back on it. Never let a woman treat you better than you treat her. Fair

exchange is no robbery. You will learn about that with time and experience also."

After his lesson of wisdom, Papa Joe got up and said good night. I looked at the clock and found we had been talking for a little over an hour. I was trying to retain as much of that information as I could but I still couldn't help but think about Linda. She was still on my mind because of all that we had shared. She was my first and I will remember this for the rest of my life.

That night I slept like a baby. The next day Granny woke me up early because she wanted the 411 on how the party was. I'm afraid of what her reaction would have been if she knew the truth.

"Sleepy head tell me all about last night. How was the party?"

"It was okay."

"Just okay."

"Well I really don't have anything to compare the party to considering it was my first real social outing."

"We'll have to make sure you have many more." The phone rang. The bell saved me. I walked out of the room to prepare myself to take a bath. After getting dressed I went outside to help pop. I was hungry but I knew Granny would call us in when breakfast was ready. It was a ritual for us to have breakfast on Saturday mornings. I was as happy as a bug in a rug to be able to spend some time eating breakfast as a family. I don't know how happy that was but pop always said that.

"What are your plans today Will?" The facetious smile on his face said you know exactly what I mean.

"I don't have much of anything planned today. My only plans were to help you."

"Why don't you call your friend and thank her for inviting you to her party? It will show her how much you appreciated the invitation." Pop and I took a drive to a nearby store. Just before we entered the store he handed me $15.00 and told me to get Linda a small box of candy as a token of appreciation.

"Remember to never take more than you give back. It's the code of ethics of real men." As we walked into the house Granny had finished preparing breakfast and I was starving.

After breakfast, I called Linda to find out if it was okay to drop by her house for a while. She said it was okay. The tone of her voice said she wanted to see me. When I arrived her mother answered the door. She was a dark skinned woman who looked to be in her 40s. I would guess she was a little bit overweight judging by her height and weight. She was short in comparison to mom, who was very tall, and appeared to be about 5'2" In my mind I call short women samples. "Have a seat James. Linda will be right down."

When Linda came down she looked different from what I had seen before. She was smiling when she stepped into the room. I wondered why.

"Hi, James. What's up?" I could see she wasn't wearing any make up. She actually looked better without it. She was very cute. This look gave her an innocent appearance, which was why it was hard to believe how much she was so into sex and lusting after men. I guess it was a phase that she was going through. We went into the living room where I pulled the box out of my pocket and presented it to her. When she opened it she was so touched that she started crying. I thought I had done something wrong. This made me nervous and I thought about leaving but she stopped me before I could move a muscle.

"James, you didn't do anything wrong. This is so sweet of you. No one has ever bought me anything. You really didn't have to do this."

"I wanted to. Linda I think you are a nice person and I really like you as a friend."

"James before we become more involved with each other I want you to know that I am involved with someone else."

"Don? The guy who's older than both you and me?"

"Yes. I didn't intend for you to find out this way. It just happened. It has nothing to do with you. How did you know that I liked chocolate turtles?" she asked, changing the subject. I smiled although I was somewhat disappointed because what my family told me had just been confirmed. I chalked this information up as experience, and realized that I must not take everything so seriously. We are only teenagers and we are far from settling down.

"Papa Joe said you can't go wrong if you get the best chocolate even if she might not like it. She will most likely appreciate it even if it might not be what she expected. If she doesn't appreciate it, she is just spoiled or just don't know the difference."

Linda was asking if we could go to the movies on Sunday after church. She said that Don would probably be entertaining the woman he was shacked up with. My first thought was that this man had the better of two worlds.

"James, I've heard some of the stuff they have been saying about me at school but I have never slept with any of the boys there regardless of what they say. I fooled around with Mr. Gerald a few times just letting him rub my breasts and feel between my legs (which made his day). You see older men tend to treat females better than younger men. You don't really have to ask for anything because they don't mind giving it to you. They want you to look good and smell good."

"Linda let me stop you right there. I don't have a full time job and I can't spend a lot of money on you. I can't compete with those guys. I only work a few evenings a week and maybe some weekends."

"Willie James Bradshaw, I didn't ask you for anything but your time." She was getting perturbed because I was jumping to conclusions. I was curious as to why she was with someone as young as me if an older man would treat her so much better. This theory didn't seem to hold true for Don who was shacked up with another woman but I kept this bit of information to myself.

"I'm sorry. I didn't mean to upset you. I apologize." Mama said never be too proud to admit when you are wrong. "I would love to take you to the movies tomorrow after church." She smiled at me. I was glad I could put her in a better mood. She kissed me before I left to go home. Upon getting home I told Papa Joe all about my visit to Linda's house. He smiled and gave me a $20.00 bill. I told him that I had a few dollars saved up for when I would purchase a good basketball.

"Keep your money and take this twenty. Now go and let your Granny know that you have a date." I couldn't believe that I was going to see Linda again. This two-week holiday vacation was starting off on the right foot.

It was Sunday and I was getting ready for church. I couldn't get Linda off of my mind. Church ended around 1:30 p.m. and I couldn't wait to get home so I could change clothes. I pulled off my suit and put on some dress pants and a casual shirt. My pants were pretty high above my waist just like Uncle Mark wears his. My intention was to keep up with all the current styles because I have a reputation to maintain. I kept my hair cut very low because of its reddish color. I often wished it was black. In other words my hair is reddish and there's nothing I can do to change that. I was always being teased about it so I kept it cut low. I was practically bald but no one seems to notice it as much. I searched the closet for my best coat and looked in the mirror. I actually looked good.

Linda was in her mother's car when she arrived at my house. She looked great. Her style and color complimented mine. It was nice to see her dress fitting so snugly because it revealed her beautifully shaped body. I knew I had enough money in my pocket because Granny had slipped me an additional $10.00 in addition to the $20.00 that pop had already given me. I knew we wouldn't spend $30.00. She couldn't possibly be able to eat that much food.

"James, why didn't you tell me that your birthday was on the 25th of the month? Maybe we could have celebrated by going out? What are we going to see at the movies?" I didn't tell her but I wanted to see a Western or horror film. Those are my favorite. It was almost as if she was reading my mind.

"There is a Western playing at the Almo." We didn't have but two movie theaters. She parked the car down by The Jack Lane, a café where most of the teenage girls and older men hung out. We walked to the corner. I saw WJ's car, which meant he was in the club probably hanging all over someone's woman. I didn't acknowledge it. I just played it cool. I knew Linda had heard about my old man's reputation. Almost everyone knew. After paying for the movie we ordered popcorn, two burgers and a coke. We chose seats that were in a dark corner. By the time we got our coats off and got comfortable, Linda kissed me on the ear. My thought was this girl knew where all my hot spots were located but I wanted to exercise a little bit more control this time. I decided I was going to call the shots.

"Come on baby let's eat. I'm starving. I haven't eaten anything all day." She calmed down so that we could eat and watch the movie. After a while she was all over me again. I then put my hand on her shoulder trying to expose my sensitive side.

"Linda you don't have to do this. I am happy just sitting here with you. Every time we get together we don't have to be all over each other or make love. Linda you are a very attractive young lady. You don't have to sleep with a guy in order for him to be with you. Don't short change yourself." When I took a closer look at her she had tears in her eyes.

"Every time I see Don or we get together we have sex and then he wants to go home. I guess I assumed that you would be the same." I took a long look at her and looked deep into her eyes. I've been told that the eyes are the windows of the soul. All I saw was a little girl afraid of rejection. "James, you are the youngest guy I have ever talked to and you are the smartest man I know." That night Linda and I became close friends. I am not going to say we didn't make love because we did but it was mutual because of the physical attraction between us. We both wanted it and neither of us felt she was using her body just for my pleasures.

That was a wonderful year. After school was out we moved back to the city with our parents. Linda was very sad at hearing this news because that would mean some distance would be put between us. I told her to keep her head up and her dress down.

After about a year of staying with my parents again I was beginning to hate where we lived. We lived in what was called Lincoln Additional, which was about ten blocks from Washington Additional. I was in junior high school and on the basketball team. I was getting better and better at the game. I still worked part time, went to school, and helped to look after my younger siblings. Daddy still had not given up on thinking I would make a career out of repairing cars. Time passed rapidly.

.........*Two and ½ Years Later*...........

I was in the tenth grade standing at 6'2" and 170 lbs. All of which were muscles that I had personally built up over time. My father was on my back day in and day out. He wanted me to go to different locations with him to assist him in repairing cars. He was still on that kick about me succeeding and making money servicing cars. My future in his eyes depended on mastering the art of repairing cars. I was very good at it but I hated it. My thing was school, work, and basketball practice. My mother would sometimes ask me to go to church with her on Sundays, which prevented him from asking for my help. In doing so I met Buck and Rob. Buck was tall, skinny, and thought he was the woman's pet and a man's friend. He would say nine out of every ten women wanted him and the other one had a problem.

Rob was the total opposite. He was shy around girls but he would try to talk to them on occasion. He confided in me that he was a virgin. There was a young lady named Mamie that was crazy about him. He said she had done everything to him short of raping him. My current lady's name was Betty. I hated going to her house because I always had to fight her mother off especially when I sat at her table. The woman was always trying to rub up against me with her breasts. I could see the embarrassment and hurt in Betty's eyes the one time she caught her trying to do it. Everyone was always saying how cute and fine her mother was. It wasn't far from the truth. These two looked more like sisters than mother and daughter. Betty was a knockout but she didn't have her mother's confidence. She was tall with light golden brown skin and was built like a coke bottle. She had Tina Turner's legs. In my opinion Betty's mom had physical features, which indicated that she was mixed with something but I didn't ask her about it. Buck said Betty was too black for him. I never really focused on a girl's skin color because other things are more important like the person and what's inside. Buck liked light skinned or damn near white girls. Rob and I liked women who were short, tall, big, small, black, pink, or blue. They all had one thing in common, which was they were a big old good one or a good old big one. It's all-good to me, as if I was actually an expert in this area. I had been with one other girl besides Linda. No one knew she was married to a friend of the family and I wanted to keep it that way. Rob and Buck thought of me as a womanizer.

LAZY SATURDAY

About two weeks later, I phoned Betty and told her I was coming over. It was a slow Saturday so I didn't have a lot of work to do. I had to catch the bus, but I was currently saving my money to purchase my own car. Two hundred fifty more dollars would put me at a dealership to negotiate the purchase of my first car. When I knocked on Betty's door her mother answered.

"Hi James. I'm sorry but you just missed Betty."

"How could that be? I just talked to her and told her I was coming over." I was trying to suppress my disappointment.

"Oh yes. I know but I have a terrible headache so I sent her to the mall to drop off my prescription and asked that she wait for it." Right away I understood what the noise was that I heard earlier on the phone.

I believe she had been listening in on our conversation.

"Why don't you come in and make yourself comfortable. I will be right back." She walked toward her bedroom. "How old are you James?"

"Presently, I'm 16." I left the half off because I wanted her to know how young I was so she would know if she came on to me she would be robbing the cradle. Her behavior in the past was an indication that I needed to be cautious.

"Oh. I am only 13 years older than you are." She returned in a white blouse and black pants so tight that I knew she had struggled to put them on. "James, I find you very attractive." Mrs. Moore was from New York and she was different from the women of the South. She would do things that no woman black or white would do and get away with it. She was what they called forward. "So young man tell me what do you see in my daughter? I see you as the type of man that needs a real woman not a child."

"A child? Betty and I are the same age. The way I see it, we are both children." I was thinking about what Papa Joe said about girls being more mature than boys. "Mrs. Moore what are you getting at?" I could be straightforward when I really wanted to. Because of my straightforwardness my mother was afraid of the way I talked to people particularly whites. I got a real kick out of looking them straight in the eyes just to see them get fidgety especially, the women and often they would turn away from me.

"What I am getting at is I would like to see you in a more private setting."

"Mrs. Moore I really like your daughter. Can't you find a man closer to your age for yourself?"

"Please call me Marie. Mrs. Moore makes me sound so old." I knew she hated when people called her Mrs. Moore, I said it on purpose. I wanted her to be reminded of her age so she could leave me alone.

"Mrs. Moore, I like Betty and I want to continue seeing her."

"What's stopping you? I wouldn't stand in the way."

"I know you don't think I'm going to see you and Betty at the same time."

"Now that I think of it, it wouldn't be such a bad idea." I couldn't believe what I was hearing. Either I was hearing things or this was the worst mother on earth. "All I want is to be good to you and maybe help you get the kind of car you want. Betty told me that you only need $250.00 more and you can buy your first car. I can give you that amount of money right now. What Betty doesn't know won't hurt her." I just stood there staring at her because I was completely shocked.

"Mrs. Moore you're right she will never know but I will. I will admit you are fine but I really do like Betty. She is a very nice girl. I wouldn't do anything to hurt her and besides, I couldn't live with myself. As for the money, I can wait because I'd rather work for it."

"Are you sure about that?" She began pulling five one hundred dollar bills out of her pocket." I couldn't believe my eyes.

"Yes I'm sure." My timing was good because I saw Betty walking in the door. The bell saved me. Her timing was everything.

"What's going on?" She was smiling and looking directly at me. I was hoping she didn't suspect anything because if I had to answer any questions about what just happened I wouldn't know whether to lie or tell the truth. Either way I didn't want to hurt Betty's feelings.

"Oh nothing honey. Did you get the medication for your mother?"

"Yes. Mom here it is. I hope you feel better." After taking her medication from Betty she went back to her bedroom. I was totally relieved.

"I was afraid I was going to miss you. After all this was a last minute thing after I talked to you."

"Yes I know. You didn't have to worry. I was going to wait for you anyway."

"So what do you have up your sleeve?"

"Why don't we see a movie?"

"Okay." Betty was into horror movies. At 17, she had full use of her mother's car. Mrs. Moore came back into the room smiling which unsettled me.

"You kids have fun." While sitting in the car Betty asked me this unusual question.

"James did my mother come on to you?" She hadn't started the car because she was waiting for my answer. "Well did she?"

"Betty you know your mom is just a flirt. I'm sure she's harmless. Everyone knows that, right? Her bark is worse than her bite." Betty started laughing. This situation was getting to be a little too weird for my taste.

"James, you have pulled her whole card. You passed her test. She told me she was going to come on to you and offer you money for your car. She obviously did from the look on your face." I don't think Betty really knew her mother because she has done this before. How many tests must a man take before he is considered okay?

"Did you and your mother plan to set me up?" I was beginning to get upset because there was nothing funny about being set up like that. I was caught totally off guard.

"Don't be mad. My mother is a little paranoid. She caught my father with one of her friends so she has very little trust in men whether they are old or young. She thinks you're a nice guy but she wanted to see what your intentions toward me are."

I could hear my mother saying you don't have to prove anything to anybody. People can see the good in you naturally. Although her mother was a little weird for what she did I decided to let it go. I smiled at Betty and gave her a kiss. Right then I was thanking God that I learned very early in life not to let money control my way of thinking. We went to the movies and had a good time.

MY BIRTHDAY

Today is November 25, which is my birthday. Betty and I have a date planned. I now have a car so we go everywhere together. Sometimes I hang out with Buck and Rob but mostly with Rob because we had more in common. Rob was dating a girl named Louise. She had him pussy whipped. The girl was two years older then him and we knew what Rob wanted and needed. There was one stipulation. No education and good grades; no Louise. He worked his butt off in school just so his needs could be met. Louise had her sights set on becoming a doctor and nothing was going to stand in her way. Rob was looking at a sure academic scholarship himself but hasn't decided what he wants to be. I worked hard because I wanted something out of life too but my scholarship would probably come from sports. I was an average student academically but an excellent student in sports. Betty told me early on that she had something special planned for my birthday. I didn't want a party but Betty, Mrs. Ida (my mother), and Mrs. Moore just wouldn't take no for an answer. We had a huge turn out for the party and everyone had a good time including me of course. I went out of my way to show my appreciation for a party that was well planned.

Betty continued to say she still had my gift and was waiting until the time was right to give it to me.

After everyone went home and we dropped my mother off, Betty stayed in the back seat while I parked in back of her house. I looked back at her and she was wearing nothing but a smile and a look on her face that said, "Take me. I'm yours." I couldn't say anything. I looked up at what appeared to be her mother's bedroom window and saw that the lights were on. I knew she was still up waiting for Betty to come in. "What if your mother sees us? What will she do to me?"

"It's what I am going to do to you if you don't get back here. I am cold!" I started the motor and pulled closer to her house out of the direct view of her mother's window. She didn't have to ask me twice to join her in the back seat. I might be nice but I am still a man and I wanted Betty more than I wanted life itself. We had been dating for a year and a half and we had come close to doing it but we never went all the way. Betty was so lovely and I was shaking like a leaf. We started kissing each other with a passion that could not be denied. I knew Betty was a virgin and I wanted to be careful with her. I couldn't get my pants off fast enough and I was scared out of my mind for the first time since being with Linda and the married woman. We had kissed before but this was something entirely different. Her lips were like honey. Betty was kissing me with an urgency that was causing my head to spin. I entered her slowly to avoid hurting her. I knew it would be painful for her since this was her first experience. I felt as if the earth was moving in slow motion and I didn't want it stop. It felt as if we were trying to merge with each other's soul. God I really love this girl. I would do just about anything for her. When we climaxed I felt at that moment that this was the girl that I would spend the rest of my life with. When I looked at Betty, she was crying and I was confused. As gently as possible I asked her what was wrong. She just kissed me again. We sat there for about half an hour holding each other and not saying anything. We were lost in our own thoughts. The second time around was even better. This time we decided against using protection. I really didn't want to use protection so that I could experience Betty without the obstacle of a condom. I know we should have but we both were willing to take the risk. It was around 1:00 a.m. when I walked Betty to her door and then I went home. My first thought was I had a nice party and the woman of my dreams, so what more could a poor guy ask for? I saw Betty everyday at school. We would eat lunch together and talk. Although I was working nights packing shelves at A & P, Betty and I got together almost every weekend.

CHRISTMAS AT GRANNY'S HOUSE

By December 20, I had given Betty, Mrs. Moore and Mom their Christmas gifts. I bought Betty a watch, Mrs. Moore a lovely scarf, and I gave Mom money.

She could always use that. I decided to spend Christmas with Pop & Granny. I had also purchased gifts for them. Pop and I had a lot of catching up to do. I had a week of work ahead of me. I told Papa Joe and Uncle Mark all about my birthday. Pop had reason to be concerned about some of the things I shared with them. I heard that Linda had gotten married to some old guy and moved away.

"Willie remember to always accept responsibility for your actions." I knew he was referring to my having unprotected sex with Betty. We had a good time and I gained at least 4 pounds from all the food I ate. A few weeks before the flu took a serious toll on my body and caused me to suffer tremendous weight loss. Granny said I needed a few pounds added to my body after losing so much weight. I now weighed 156 pounds. I came home that Monday after Christmas. The first thing I did was called Betty to let her know that I was back in town.

"Oh James, I am so glad you're back. Did you have fun?"

"Yes I did."

"Did you run into your old girlfriend, Linda?"

"Of course not. I told you that Linda lives in Chicago now. Do I detect a hint of jealousy baby? You know that you're the only woman for me." I could picture her smiling and twisting her hair around her finger, which was a habit. "Betty, stop twisting your hair." She laughed.

"You know me only too well."

SLEEPING IN THE BED I MADE

Everything was going well until February, when we were all excited because graduation was near and going away to college would follow after that. We had just celebrated Betty's birthday. I had two scholarships on my belt: one from basketball and the other from tennis. I was the best in my school (so everyone said). The coach commented that I had a very bright future ahead of me.

It was about 1:00 p.m. Rob, Buck and I were horsing around. I saw Betty across the gym when she first walked in. Right away my heart was in my stomach. I could tell she had been crying and the guys picked up on it also. Right then I couldn't move. Finally, Rob brought me back to reality.

"James man you had better check on your woman." I walked up to her and my mouth was so dry that words couldn't find their way out. I could see Ms. Katz, the gym teacher, out of the corner of my eye. It was no secret that she hated the male race. As I got closer she gave me a dirty look and walked away. I don't think she even liked male dogs and cats.

"Betty what's wrong?" The tears started flowing again but harder than before. I put my arms around her to lead her away from the others. My teacher was in the doorway. She was nice enough to give me the okay to miss my next class. It seemed as if everyone knew what was going on but me. We were sitting in the lunchroom a few minutes later.

"Now Betty will you please talk to me. Whatever hurts you, hurts me too."

"James please don't hate me because I didn't mean for this to happen. I know we have so many plans for college but I'm… I'm three months pregnant." My mind went back to the night of my birthday when we made love for the second time without using protection. I knew that was when it happened. "James please say something."

"Betty calm down. It's not the end of the world and you are not the first 18-year-old girl to get pregnant. We will think of something. Have you told your mother?"

"No. She will kill us."

"No she won't because she would then land herself in a jail cell." I was trying to humor her so she would remain calm.

"James this is no time for jokes!!" She snapped at me.

"Betty, pull yourself together." I didn't want to show my disappointment. "Let's go and tell your mother about this now and maybe she will be able to guide us toward making the right decision." Before we could get to the door it opened and Marie was standing there looking puzzled.

"What are you two doing out of school so early?" I decided to speak first because Betty looked as if she was falling apart.

"Mrs. Moore…"

"Marie." She sounded very cold.

"Marie, Betty and I have a problem we need to talk to you about."

"Can it wait?" We shook our heads to indicate that no it couldn't wait. "What is it?" She had fear in her voice and eyes by now.

"Mama, I'm pregnant. I'm so sorry. Please don't be mad at James or me. We thought we were being careful."

"Careful? You mean you guys are having sex? Did it happen more than once?"

"Yes, it happened on more than one occasion but only once without protection."

"You have now found out that it only takes one time without protection to conceive a baby!" She was screaming at the top of her lungs.

"Marie I am more to blame than Betty!"

"Oh no one is to blame. Pregnancy is the result when you don't use a condom. How far along are you?"

"I am three months pregnant. Maybe 10 weeks."

"Why didn't you tell someone sooner?"

"I was afraid and I wasn't sure!!"

"Maybe we can still take care of it. I'll call my doctor. If he can't do it then he will recommend someone who can." What was she talking about? I know she didn't think for one second that I would want to abort my child. I know I wasn't smart when I got Betty pregnant but hell will freeze over before I let my child be aborted.

"Wait a minute. What are you saying that you want her to have an abortion?"

"Do you have a better plan?"

"Yes. Please don't think of taking her to the abortion clinic. I will give up both of my scholarships and get a job after graduation. Just please don't make her abort our baby." I can't explain the fear and hurt I was feeling. Tears started rolling down my cheeks. "The baby is innocent. Betty if you just carry the baby to term, have it and then give it to me to raise, you will never have to worry about it again. You can give it my name. As an alternative, we could get married to give the baby a proper home with both parents. I have medical insurance on my job." Betty's mother thought I was going out of my mind making all these grown-up decisions.

"James does your mother and father know anything about this?"

"No, but I know my mother will back me on my decision and help me out. I know she will. My mechanism of support exists in my mother and my grandparents."

"I'll tell you what. Let's go and talk to your parents."

"My mother won't be home until 4:00 p.m. It's only 2:45 p.m. now." We waited out the time. Later on Betty wasn't feeling well.

"My head is hurting and I feel as if the weight of the world is on my shoulders. May I have some water please?" Marie went to the kitchen for me. My tongue felt as if there was sawdust on it. I was completely at a lost for words. We sat around making small talk. At 4:00 p.m. we were on our way to my house. Mama came to the door with one of those all too familiar looks of hers. This one said "James what have you done?" Before we could get half way inside my house, Marie went into action. She had the entire story out in about 3 ½ minutes tops. The woman didn't inhale or exhale during the whole time she was talking. At the end, she got my attention.

"James thinks he can take care of this child." She was saying this with a smirk on her face. Mom spoke for the first time.

"Well now maybe he can with some family support. James is a reliable and responsible young man. There is just one problem."

"What is that?"

"We have to tell WJ. I don't know what he will say or do for that matter. He will be home around six unless he stops at the bar after work for a drink. After 7:30 came and went Marie and Betty went home. There was no WJ to be found. Mom didn't really have much to say. But after they left, she decided it was time to have a talk with me.

"James when we make our beds we have to lie in them but it's not the end of the world. I want you to know that whatever happens I am with you all the way." Mom had a way of making me feel so much better during the worse situations. Although she was disappointed in me, she gave me a big hug.

"Mom I will take care of everything. It's going to be alright." I went and took a bath while Mom reached for the phone. She was talking to Mrs. Searight. They were good friends. She said something about growing up in the same town with her. After my bath I went straight to bed for it had been a trying day. I couldn't sleep and the only thing that I could think about was Betty and school. I woke up the next morning in a cold sweat. I had dreamed I wouldn't be able to go to college. Reality had hit me at the moment that I wouldn't be able to use either of my scholarships. I made God and myself a promise that I would go to college no matter what.

When I went into the dining room that morning I knew that mom had told WJ everything. My mother (Mrs. Ida) looked as if she wanted to cry. I then knew how much I had really disappointed her. WJ showed no passion toward my current situation.

"Your mama tells me you got caught up in that Moore girl's trap." Everyone knew that WJ had a crush on Marie Moore but she made it very clear that he was not her type.

"It wasn't a trap. We just weren't careful enough."

"How do you know it's yours?"

"I know because I am the only one she has been with."

"You mean you went and spoiled yourself for a virgin?" I hated when he talked like that. "The girls in my day were smart and if they weren't they got rid of it. How many months is she any way?"

"I think it's too late to do anything about it."

"What is she going to do?" he asked.

"She will have the baby and I will raise and take care of our child." He continued to irritate me with his cold attitude and referring to my child as "it."

"She's not ready to be a mother! And you! Are you ready to be a father?"

"I don't know. I just know I have to try. By the grace of God I am going to make the best of it."

"What if she comes back in about six or seven years and wants the kid back?"

"First of all my name will be on the birth certificate as the father; also she will sign papers awarding me full custody of our child."

"That's my boy. You have a good head on your shoulders just like the men in my family." We won't go into anything regarding his family. His family was okay but none were going to win any contests when it came down to common sense and decision-making abilities. I went to work and talked to my boss. He was really counting on me going to college but he respected me more for accepting my responsibilities and not trying put the entire burden on Betty's shoulders.

It wasn't easy but we got through the summer. Betty hated me during the later months of her pregnancy. I did everything I could to make her happy but it just wasn't enough. She would let me rub her stomach and talk to the baby only when she felt up to it. I had a long talk with Papa Joe and Granny because I was concerned about Betty. They offered to let the baby and me stay with them since granny's medical condition had improved. It would be less work for Mama, my sisters, and brothers. Granny said she would keep the baby while I worked and consider taking a few night classes.

I worked like a slave. Jack Searight was the best boss. He allowed me to work all the overtime that became available. He even fixed it where Betty could put the baby under my medical plan. He went out of his way to be supportive which peaked my curiosity. His wife and my mother were friends which kind of explained why he seemed as if he wanted to be more supportive of me. While it felt good, it was a little puzzling at the same time. I had too much on my mind to really try to figure Jack out. I wouldn't take any public assistance nor would I borrow any money to make ends meet. Jack told me to concern myself only with getting things ready for the baby. Betty and Marie were sure about one thing. They didn't want a baby to be a part of their household. Betty was too young to raise a child and of course Marie had her career. Neither one gave it a second thought. I often thought about Papa Joe saying girls mature a lot faster than boys did. I think he got it backwards with our situation. Everyday Betty would act more and more like a little girl.

The big day was August 15th. When the baby was born I was right there to see it all. She went into labor that Saturday night. The baby was born around 5:45 a.m. Sunday morning. Marie had informed the doctor to give the baby to me right away. Betty was not to see or hold the baby. There was to be no chance of mother and child bonding. Mom was there to support me. I didn't need help with the baby because I had been here and done this before with my siblings.

I couldn't understand why Betty didn't try to stand up for herself after all she had just turned 18 six months ago on February 3rd. Marie always said Betty would be rich and famous and her name would appear in the spotlight. My thoughts were interrupted when I saw Mr. Searight.

"James, I came to lend you my support. How is everything?" This man had been a good boss and I felt that he was really going beyond being my boss at this point. I was so lost in my thoughts I didn't hear the nurse calling me.

"Mr. Bradshaw. Mr. Bradshaw your baby will be clean soon. You can hold him." A few minutes later, the nurses handed me the baby. He was crying and I wanted to cry too looking at this young person that couldn't do anything for himself. He was totally dependent on me. I was forced to grow up at that moment at the age of 17. I knew there was no turning back. I had stepped into a man's shoes and I would walk in these shoes for the rest of my life. I was a boy who had contributed to conceiving this child but as a man I would take care of him.

Marie was holding Betty and looking at me smiling. I was surprised she had something positive to say. "He is lovely."

My mother was glad to see him and immediately she started to dote on him. "My first grandchild. He looks just like you Mann." She started calling me Mann when I was 12. I was so proud because I saw in front of me a healthy child who had wrinkled skin, 10 toes, 10 fingers and the rest was all in its proper place. After they got him tagged, they said he would have to stay in the hospital for 24 hours just for a detailed checkup to ensure that he was okay. He went to the nursery after they tagged him Baby Bradshaw.

"What are you going to name him son? You can't call him Baby Bradshaw forever you know."

"Why not? Just kidding." We both laughed. "I will have a name for him by tomorrow." I left the hospital because I had to be at work that day. When I got there, Jack was there and he had a grin on his face that went from ear to ear. He was all right for a white guy.

"I waited around to give you a ride James but I had to get back here. I saw your car. So what did you name the baby?" At that point, I think I made up my mind.

"I'm going to name him Jackson Jeremy Bradshaw and for short he can be called J.J. What do you think?"

"You mean you are going to give him my first name?"

"Yes I thought I would name him after somebody that was cool." Jack didn't have a son and his daughter was handicapped. She would follow me around in the store. Annie was now 20 with the mind of a 10-year-old child. Jack walked around all day with his chest stuck out telling everybody that my son had his first name. I got off work around 6 p.m. I went home to take a bath and decided that I would call Betty afterwards. She sounded happy when I called.

"James my mother and I decided that we are moving back to New York."

"Betty, what about us? I thought we had something special." I had high hopes that she would come around and love the baby as much as I did.

"James it would never work between us with you insisting on keeping that baby." "That baby". I couldn't believe I was hearing these words from a woman who carried this child for 9 months.

"Betty, do you have any feelings for him at all? After all we did make him together and you carried him for 9 months?"

"He is your son." I could feel the tears forming in my eyes but I was determined to be strong. "James, I know he is better off with you or someone else who will love him. I am not ready for this type of responsibility. Besides that, you are more ready for this than I am."

"Betty, I am no more ready for this than you are, I just know that taking responsibility for my actions is the right thing to do." I was staring at the phone wondering how I could have ever loved such a cold-hearted woman. How could she carry a child for 9 months and just walk away? I've heard of men that have walked away from their children but not women. It is quite obvious that despite all the time that we spent together I really didn't know her.

I didn't sleep well that night. My mom noticed it too. "Mann you act as if you are having second thoughts about this. Oh no!"

"I'm not having second thoughts about the baby. I was just thinking how could a woman just walk away from her child?"

"I don't know how, son, but some can and they do. There are not many but a few who will." I went back to my room to get the rest of my stuff. I was moving in with Papa Joe and granny. My brothers were counting down the minutes to when I would be vacating their space. I put the rest of my stuff in my car. I was prepared to pick up J.J. The nurses were very nice and they couldn't give me enough advice on childcare. I received about 10 phone numbers from people at the hospital who wanted to help when I needed them, mostly women.

I took Liz, my oldest sister, with me to pick up J.J. She is going to spend a few days with us also. By the time we got to granny's house I was dog-tired. I got the baby settled in first. I asked Liz to watch him until I made a quick run. My destination was Betty's house only to find the movers packing up the rest of their belongings. They had already left without saying good-bye. I went home, picked Liz up, dropped her off at work, and returned back home to stare at the walls.

Jack changed my hours to 3 p.m. - 11 p.m. as a favor to me. That would give me the opportunity to take classes during the day instead of at night and still be able to spend some time with J.J. This arrangement wasn't easy on my family but Liz, Granny and Pop were a big help.

My Aunt Mable worked for the Public Aid Office. She wanted to help me get benefits for my son but I rejected the idea. I refused to take any handouts. She talked me into applying for grants to support my education, which turned out to be a big benefit. Part of the grant went toward paying Granny to baby sit J.J. I was enrolled in Hinds Junior College where I was a double major, majoring in Education and Management.

Although I had a full schedule, I always had time for my son. I watched as J.J.'s first teeth came in and when he took his first steps. He was growing so fast it appeared as if every month I was at the store buying new clothes and shoes to replace the old ones that no longer fit.

UNEXPECTED CHANGES

J.J. was 22 months old when Granny got sick. She died August 3rd, just 12 days before J.J.'s second birthday. Papa Joe was devastated at her passing away. During the months after her death he wasted away to little or nothing. He only lived five months following granny's death and was buried next to her. I was out of school during this time and had plans to attend Jackson State University. Just as I was about to put my life back together, tragedy came knocking on my door again when Jack suffered a heart attack. Although he survived, they decided to sell the store and move to Florida. I was nineteen, homeless, out of a job, and had a two-year-old son to care for. I had the same feelings I had when Betty first told me she was pregnant. I didn't know what to do. Granny's words of wisdom continued to stay on my mind. She always said prayer would change things. At that moment I got down on my knees and prayed. I didn't really know how I knew but I felt that God heard me.

The next day I got up with a clear head and I suddenly knew what I had to do. I asked my mother and Liz if they would take care of J.J. for the two-year duration that I would be in the army. Mom just about had a heart attack thinking about the Vietnam War and all. I had made up my mind to go for the sake of my child. The two years went pretty fast as I was on a mission to get in and out for the future of my son. I got a good trade in the service as a physician's assistant and with a little more work I could have been a doctor.

SURPRISING NEWS AND AN UNEXPECTED GIFT

After I returned home I was told that Mrs. Searight had been trying to get in touch with me for the last month or so. She called and wrote my mother on a regular basis. It's been two years since I last saw them. I kept in touch with them by phone and letters but all of a sudden the communication stopped.

I called the number my mother had written down and Mrs. Searight answered on the first ring.

"Hello."

"Mrs. Searight please."

"James is that you?"

"Yes ma'am it is. How are you and the family?"

"James, Jack died about four months ago. Annie was placed in a group home that will take very good care of her and she is getting better. James, I am sick and tired but I must see you as soon as possible. Jack made me promise I would get in touch with you if something happened to him before he could see you himself. How soon can you come to Florida? The sooner the better." J.J. was sitting comfortably in my arms and I was disappointed at the thought of having to tell him that I have to go away again. I asked Mom if I should take him with me. She decided that three more days away would not make much of a difference. I kissed my son and had Mom drop me off at the bus station. After flying 20 hours to get home there was no way was I getting back on a plane to fly to Florida. I had jet lag as it was so I decided to take a bus ride. I arrived in Tampa Bay, Florida 10 hours after the bus hit the road. There was no doubt in my mind that I would be flying back because the bus ride was hard on my legs, back and buttocks. I took a cab to Mrs. Searight's house. Come to think of it, I never knew her first name simply because I never bothered to ask. This was my first trip to Florida and most likely the last. Mrs. Searight answered the door.

"James, come in honey. How are you? My, my, you are a fine young man. Jack would have been so proud of you." She had a black housekeeper who was standing in the kitchen doorway looking as if she would kill me if I made the wrong move. She stepped into the room.

"Helen, I want you to meet James. This is the young man Jack was always talking about. He is J.J.'s father."

"Oh, the baby in the pictures?" They looked at each other with a smile.

"Yes."

"Hi. I am sorry for staring so hard but I am not used to white people talking about someone of color as if they are a part of the family."

"It's okay. I understand." She was very pretty. I was so mesmerized by her beauty that only Mrs. Searight's voice interrupted my thoughts.

"James, can you spend the night and return home tomorrow or the next day? We have some business to take care of and the banks are closing in about an hour. It's important that we go tomorrow. You can stay right here. You may use Annie's room. Helen has her own room. We can add another place setting for you for dinner." I really didn't want to stay there but I guess with Helen being there it was okay. This was the 1970's and we had come from being colored to being black. I was a black man and this was a white woman's house. I had to be careful. The last time I looked Florida was still located in the south. It wasn't any better north, east or west as far as how blacks were treated but the south was the worst of them all. The only difference between locations was that there was just a different type of prejudice. Mrs. Searight wasn't about to take no for an answer so I said yes.

After dinner that evening, we sat around talking until about 8:30 p.m. Mrs. Searight then excused herself. Helen and I talked and discovered we had a lot in common. She was 26 and I was 21 ½. Sometimes I felt 50 when you consider everything that I have been through. Helen had no children and she was taking two correspondence courses in nursing. Next year she would be doing clinical two days out of the week. She started working for the Searights right after they moved to Florida. They hit it off good after she responded to an ad placed in the newspaper. They were paying for her education so she had nothing to complain about. I checked my watch to see if it was 9:45 Eastern Standard Time (E.S.T.) I hadn't been in bed in 28 ½ hours considering the time change.

"There is one thing I would like to do and that is take a bath."

"Follow me. Everything you need is already in the bathroom." She was true to her word. I had available to me a pair of pajamas, towels, and a razor. After I got cleaned up and ready for bed, I said good night and closed my door. I don't remember lying down I was so sleepy.

FAMILY SECRETS

I got up at seven and they were both in the kitchen. I took a quick shower and joined them. Helen cooked a feast. The woman could really "burn." Mrs. Searight wanted me to see all the new pictures of J.J. I discovered that she had some I didn't have. Mom had kept her up to date on the development of J.J. They really kept in touch with each other. It appeared that they were closer than before.

"James take your time and eat some breakfast. In the meantime I will get ready so we can take care of some unfinished business." She acted as if this was a matter of life and death. She continued to mention something to the tune of keeping her promise to Jack. "Helen will drive us."

Everyone at the bank knew her and Helen. This nice lady approached us from out of nowhere to speak to Mrs. Searight and then Helen.

"Good morning Helen, Mrs. Searight." She didn't know me at all but she took the liberty to speak.

"Hi, Rachel. This is James Bradshaw or shall I say Willie James Bradshaw. He worked for my husband."

"Well Mr. Bradshaw I've heard so much about you. I feel as if I know you already. Step right this way and have a seat." She went to retrieve some documents that required signatures. "Now I need both of you to sign some papers as the letter explained." I was looking a bit puzzled because I had no idea what she was talking about.

"Oh James from the look on your face you didn't get the last letter from Jack."

"I don't know. The last one I received was sometime in February if I recall."

"Oh no. A letter was sent to you from the bank in April. I assumed you knew why you were here."

"No ma'am. I thought you had something to discuss with me."

"No. Honey, I am so sorry. You must have thought I was crazy. We couldn't read the will until you were present. Jack put you, Helen, Annie, J.J., and me in the will." I was asking myself why J.J. and me would be in Jack's will. We weren't a part of his family. He was like a father to me at times but that was work related. At the same time, I couldn't understand what was going on this very moment. A white man put me and my son in his will.

"The only way any assets could be released from Jack's estate was if the others were declared legally dead, in another continent, or couldn't be located. In addition, he left a letter for you that no one else would be allowed to read. If we couldn't get in contact with you it was to be destroyed and never read by anyone else."

I was standing there looking like a fool. Look up lost in the dictionary and you would find my picture right there. Mrs. Searight took me by the hand and led me to a seat. They got the safety deposit box and sure enough there was the will and a sealed letter addressed to me along with a set of instructions in the event that I didn't make it back from the service. I took the letter with unsteady hands. All eyes were on me and I was just as curious as they were. Everyone wanted to know what was so important about this letter that no one else could read it but me. The bank representative spoke first.

"Would you like some privacy Mr. Bradshaw?"

"Yes please. Thank you." My hands were wet and I could feel the sweat on my forehead. I was still in my uniform and boy was it getting a little hot.

"Come with me." I was escorted to a private room. I opened the envelope only to find a second envelope. Jack was really serious about the privacy of this letter. The second envelope read Willie James Bradshaw Only. I opened the letter and sat down. Its contents were:

Hi James. If you are reading this letter then I have passed away and you made it back safely from the service, thank God. I am happy about that. James, I am sorry that I couldn't tell you this face to face, man to man, years ago but Marie made me promise not to. Yes, James, Marie Moore. Marie was my first child. Her mother was of African dissent and I loved her with all my heart. When she got pregnant, she moved to New York. I was only seventeen at the time. Being in Mississippi during a time when desegregation was not popular, a white boy and a colored girl could not make it together. We kept things on the down low for our safety. My father made me promise to always look out for her and make sure she was taken care of. I knew that meant J.J. too. J.J. is my only great grandchild. Kathy doesn't know about any of this and I want to keep it that way. It would be okay to share this information if and only if she passes away before you, only then. There would be nothing to gain from hurting her. She loves you like a son and she would die for J.J. James, I wanted to tell you all of this when you gave J.J. my first name. I was so happy that I could have jumped out of my clothes. I wasn't a rich man but I made a good living and my father left me financially stable in his will. The enclosed $25,000 cash is for you. The trust fund was set up for J.J. with an initial investment of $10,000. It may not be much now but by the time he is ready for college, he will have more than enough money to finance his education.

I just sat there thinking about both Marie & Betty. A lot of things that didn't make sense to me before started falling into place. For example, why was Marie so light skinned? Why did I walk in on her and Jack in a heated argument? I had just assumed it was over a purchase or something. I knew Marie's mother was from Jackson, Mississippi, but she was born and raised in New York City. Her mother had died before they moved back to Mississippi. Betty said Marie got her color from her father and that explains why J.J. was so light especially when he was first born. Now he has a cocoa brown complexion with green eyes. It's funny now that I think of it. They never really said if Marie's father was dead or alive which was strange. Betty would change the subject but she did say once that her grandmother died from a broken heart. She didn't marry Marie's father so she never married anyone. Moore was her maiden name. Marie never used her married name. I picked the letter up again to finish reading it.

James, I wanted to tell you the truth when Betty got pregnant but Marie said she would make Betty have an abortion or move away and give the baby up for adoption. Marie never forgave me for refusing to run away and marry her mother. She said that because I was white I could have done anything I wanted to, including marrying her mother. It really wasn't that simple. I didn't want Marie to have her way so I paid her $30,000 to let Betty have the baby so you could get full custody of him. That way I could watch J.J. grow up. Then I had a heart attack, which changed everything. Your mother kept in contact with us through phone calls and pictures, which allowed us to be able to watch J.J. grow up. James try not to be disappointed in me. I only did what I thought was best for everyone. Please find it in your heart to take care of Kathy and Helen for me. I know I am asking for a lot but you will have to relocate. They really need you very much. Please put this letter away for J.J. someday so he will know and understand his great grandfather.

I had to sit down and get my thoughts together. This was a lot to lie on a 21-year-old man. I put the letter in my pocket and walked out of the room. All eyes were on me. Mrs. Searight and Helen approached me out of concern for me.

"Are you okay? You look as if you saw a ghost."

"Oh yes. I'm okay." I might have.

"The will needs to be read and then our business will be finished." The lawyer was ready for the reading of the will. I could see the shock on his face when I walked into the room. Jack never used color to describe people. He talked as if everyone was the same so these people assumed I was white. Most were curious as to what my ties were with these white people. I was a little too dark for them even with my red hair. I couldn't possibly be related. The lawyer dismissed his thoughts and began reading the will.

Annie would be taken care of for the rest of her life. Mrs. Searight had nothing to worry about because he left her financially stable. For me, he left the house in Florida, which was basically paid for. My only responsibility was to move in and pay the annual property taxes. There was some property that was left to some friends in Jackson. Their names were not disclosed but I knew it was Betty and Marie he was referring to. This land was to never be sold off so J.J. would have a home when he becomes an adult. Kathy never commented on what she heard.

DECISIONS, DECISIONS, DECISIONS

It was noon before we could get away from the bank. I was hungry and my head was killing me. I had so many thoughts running through my mind.

We went back to the Searight place and I called the airport. It would be 8:00 p.m. Before I could get a flight going back to Jackson. It was Helen who broke the silence.

"I am going to fix us something to eat. I am starving. James what would you like, a burger or hot dogs?"

"Anything will do. Thank you."

"James, you seem worried. Is there something wrong? Was the letter bad news?"

"Not really. It allowed me to piece a few things together that was puzzling at first and a little hard to understand. Jack asked me to look out for you, Annie, and Helen."

"James why don't you move here? You have inherited a home and your mother has indicated that she is ready to leave Jackson." Jack did tell her about the house.

"I can't move here, at least not right now. I haven't even been home because it was urgent that I be here. I didn't spend two hours in Jackson. I need time to think about all this. My main priority right now is to spend some time with my family. Right then I noticed a change in my voice." The more I talked the louder my voice was and this scared Kathy and Helen. I could see fear in both their eyes. I tried to calm myself down. "I am sorry. I am so sorry. Please forgive me. I just have to think about this. Right now I am going for a walk." Their house was only two blocks from the ocean. I always think well when I am watching the movement of the water. My thoughts went to my mother, J.J. and my siblings, which was my family that was waiting for me back in Mississippi. They were the only things keeping me in Jackson. So many thoughts went through my mind that I lost track of time. I looked at my watch and it said 3:30 p.m. I had to get back because I knew that if I stayed out any longer they would be worried about me. I was starving and I needed food. Just as I arrived, the door opened. It was Mrs. Searight with a smile on her face.

"I am really hungry Mrs. Searight." Helen was listening as I rubbed my stomach.

"James please, please call me Kathy."

"Come on. I prepared something you might like. I know you have to be getting back to Mississippi but can you stay just one more night? I just would like to talk to you more. Maybe if you look around it might persuade you to reconsider."

"I would have to cancel my flight but I don't think it would be a problem."

"Okay. Give me the number to the airport." Kathy cancelled the flight while I sat down to eat. Later on we drove by the house Jack left me in his will to take a look at it. It was a very nice three-bedroom house in a mixed neighborhood. There was a fence around the backyard and a school across the street. Jack thought of everything. He made it almost impossible to say no to moving here. On the way back we stopped for dinner. It was time to call home after my decision to spend another day in Florida. I assumed that mom would probably be the first to get to the phone. She did but she wasn't surprised.

"When are you coming home?"

"Tomorrow."

"Are you sure?"

"Yes, I miss you all. Where is J.J.?"

"Right here."

"Hi, Daddy. I miss you. When you go away again can I go with you?"

"Yes. Whenever I go away again, you can go. I promise."

"Okay Daddy. Goodbye." He hung up the phone.

HELEN

This had been a long day. It was only 7:00 p.m. but I was exhausted. Kathy went to bed. I took a bath and did the same after saying good night to Helen. Just as I was about to dose off I heard the door open. I lay very still and waited to see who had entered my room. It was Helen.

"James! James! I need to talk to you." I turned over and moved to the opposite side of the bed so that she could sit down. I knew Kathy couldn't hear us because her bedroom was located at the back of the house. I liked Helen. She was about a size 14 or 16 and 5'8". Although she was a healthy woman, everything seems to be in the right place. She definitely was no slob. She lay down beside me.

"James it has been a long time since I've had a date or been with a man."

"Helen, Kathy is right down the hall. She might get up for something and see us."

"She has no reason to come down here. Once she goes to bed, she never comes out of her room until the following morning and besides her hearing aide needs a battery. She can't hear us considering she sleeps without it." Feeling her warm body next to mine, neither one of us said anything more. I didn't bother to tell her that I hadn't been with but three

women in the past two years and I paid for them
because I didn't want any further obligation to them.
I just love them and leave them. Helen was all over
me, which was a sure sign that she needed some
tender loving care. This was one time that I knew
what I wanted and needed. There was something
about Helen that just couldn't be denied. First she
turned the lights on which was a good sign that her
and I were on the same page. The woman was a 38D
and her skin was as soft as a baby's butt. She smelled
so good, unlike the ladies I had been with before.
They smelled okay but this was different. I wasn't
paying and I really wanted it. I didn't know women
actually sucked a man's breasts. The things she could
do with her body were completely turning me on. I
couldn't control myself and she was in total control.
I knew I was stroking it but the girl taught me how.
This was going to be a night to remember. The lady
got me off several times and she was really enjoying
herself. She even had to comment on the size of my
chocolate stick. Linda had absolutely nothing on
Helen. This woman did things to me that I couldn't
imagine. I didn't mind returning the favor either. I
wasn't the same little boy that Linda shocked years
ago. I was a man who had matured after a tour in the
service and I pride myself on making good love.
Making love to Helen was sheer enjoyment. I kissed
her from head to toe. After a few hours of making
love we were both exhausted to a point of no return.
I am not sure when Helen went back to her room

because I was out like a light. I only know that she kissed me sometime during the early morning.

I woke up to the smell of bacon, eggs, and coffee. The shower was my first destination. I felt a lot better and more relaxed then I have felt in the past year. Now I know I need a companion. They were both sitting at the table when I walked in. Kathy was smiling harder then Helen.

"Did you sleep well?"

"Yes, mam. I did. Do you mind if I take a walk before eating."

"Oh no. Go right ahead. Just be careful, son." She sounded just like my mom.

There wasn't much difference between white mothers and black mothers. They both wanted to take care of someone. I walked for about a ½ hour. I really needed to work out, but the walk was the best I could do under the circumstances. I returned to Mrs. Searight's house and ate as if food was being rationed. Just as I was getting ready to leave, Mrs. Searight offered to drive me to the airport. Helen had already made my reservation for 12:00 p.m. E.S.T. I really hated saying good-bye to Helen because I knew I would miss her. It would have been great to spend more time with her to get to know her better. If the timing was right and I was ready to enter into a relationship, I would have given us a chance. She really knows how to listen to a man. She's kind, truthful, sensitive, and she acts like a woman. In addition to all that, she seems to be secure about herself. Helen had qualities that you don't normally find in most 1970s women. We said good-bye to each other. She kissed me gently and said she would be seeing me real soon. Her smile was so beautiful it made it hard for me to leave but I had to get back to Jackson.

KATHY'S CONFESSION

On the way to the airport, Kathy said she needed to talk to me, which was why she offered to drive me in the first place. After all the news I had gotten on this trip I was hoping and praying that it wouldn't be bad news or another hidden secret.

"James the bank deposit was wired to your account in Jackson. I confirmed it this morning. J.J.'s trust fund is in the Deposit Gantry National bank. Listen I know Jack, asked you not to tell me what was in that letter and I won't ask, but I will tell you what I know. I am aware that J.J. is my great grandchild by marriage? I love him more than life itself so it doesn't matter what happened in the past. No one can take away the love I feel for that little boy. Jack has always tried to protect me even after his death. He didn't recognize my strength and treated me as if

I was a piece of glass that would shatter at any given moment. I can hold my own. Ida told me about Marie and Betty because I had found a cancelled check that listed Marie as the payee. I was upset but couldn't bring myself to ask Jack about it. I never told Jack but Ida told me all about Marie and Betty 15 years ago. Ida and I have been friends for over 30 years. We grew up in the same town. Her mother worked for my mother and we got close over the years. There was no reason to rock the boat since everything happened before I married Jack. She had a look of relief on her face. The truth was finally told after living a lie for all of these years. I know Jack sent Marie money every month but there was enough money left to go around with the store and his inheritance. He even sent Maggie money up until she died."

Once again, things started falling into place because I never knew what Marie's mother's name was either. Now I know that it was Maggie.

"I also know that they never stopped loving each other. It was difficult in the state of Mississippi for a white man to be involved with a black woman. Jack would have been ostracized and Maggie could have been hurt or even worse, killed. All of that took place in 1939 and now we sit here in 1976 where there are people who haven't changed their prejudice attitudes one bit. I just wish he had confided in me. I suspect he only wanted to protect you. He really did love you as much as he did Annie. Although he was disappointed that she wasn't born a normal child, he loved her with all his heart. Maggie gave him a perfect child and I just wasn't able to do the same."

"He never blamed you for Annie's condition. I know he didn't."

"It just hurts that he didn't trust me enough to tell me the truth. Ida trusted me enough to tell me truth and I will always love her for that. James please let me continuously be a part of J.J.'s life. Please make him aware that he has two grandmothers, Ida and myself. Please bring him around to see me and I want to come and see him." She couldn't hold back the tears nor did she care that people were watching us especially with me being a black man and her an older white woman sitting there crying in my arms. A few minutes later a fat white cop walked over and started to ask questions.

"Is she okay?"

"Yes, officer. I am fine. I was just seeing my grandson off." The man's face dropped to the floor. He walked away. I could see him looking back and I swear I saw him shake his head. Imagine what was going through his mind. He was probably thinking what is this world coming to or she must have been messing around with a black man.

"Kathy, I am sorry about all of this. If I could say anything to make it better I would. I will tell J.J. all about you. Knowing my mother he probably already knows about you." We both smiled. I was glad I could provide her with some comfort. I got out of the car and headed inside the airport.

"Take cares James. I hope to see you soon. Kiss my great grandson for me." Her words caused some heads to turn. Once again I wondered what was going through their minds to hear a white woman say those words to a black man. This thought disappeared as I went to the ticket counter to pick up my airplane ticket. As I walked to the boarding gate I realized that I had a lot to think about. There was a lot of planning to be done for J.J. and myself if I decided to move to Florida. I felt as if a lifetime had been covered with in such a short span of time. Some of the thoughts that went through my head were the fact that my son's great grandmother was white, his grandmother was $\frac{1}{2}$ white and his mother was $\frac{1}{4}$ white, but he was black but lighter than me. There was no doubt that my son was black and so was I. That was all that people would see. The plane ride was short and sweet. After only an hour and a half on the plane, Mom, J.J. and WJ greeted me at the airport. Since WJ was present very little was said in the car. There was so much I wanted to talk to Mom about, but I wanted to talk to her alone. At home, I was playing with my son, whom I had missed very much, when my mother walked into my room. WJ was gone which made everybody happy. Anytime he stayed around he would find something to complain about and I wasn't in the mood to deal with any stress from anyone.

MORE FAMILY SECRETS

"Mom, why didn't you tell me?"

"Honey the truth has a way of coming out and besides I wanted it to come from Jack. God rests his soul. He was so crazy about you. When you and Betty got together he was overjoyed. You are everything he wanted in a son. He always felt guilty about Betty. When Betty got pregnant and you wanted to keep the baby, he knew you wouldn't get the opportunity to go away to college. I guess he felt a little guilty about the situation with Maggie also. God rest her soul." Mom would always say God rest his or her soul when speaking of the dead. "The poor woman just refused to live without Jack in her life and when he married Kathy she knew she had lost him forever. He sent a great deal of money for her and Marie but he couldn't spend any significant amount of time with her. She wanted him to move up North so they could be together permanently but his life was here in Mississippi. Old Mr. Searight wasn't going for that either. He would have taken away Jack's inheritance and what would Maggie and the baby do then? Maggie lived long enough to see Betty grow up. Marie was married at the time but I don't know much about him except she caught him in bed with one of her friends. She sued him for everything he had and took her maiden name back. Marie always blamed Jack for her mother's death. She said her mother died from none other than a broken heart. The woman had a serious hate for men and she wanted all of them to pay. If J.J. had been a girl then just maybe they would have wanted him. I am not absolutely sure because that's just Ida's theory."

"What was Marie's mother's entire name?"

"Maggie Marie Moore. Marie was named after her mother. Her entire name is Jackie Marie Moore. She was named after Jack and Maggie. Jack would have died for her but she made his life a living hell. She was constantly threatening to expose him to the world or to Kathy. That's why I told Kathy I didn't want her to be hurt. I knew she would not have kept something like that from me if it involved WJ. Now you know as much as I know." Although she looked to be telling the truth, a part of me wondered what else she might be hiding. She had a way of keeping a secret about almost anything. Now I knew she even kept them from me.

MAKING ADJUSTMENTS

I got up early the next day because I had to find a place to stay. I called the bank to make sure the money had been wired to my account. With what Jack left and the money I sent Mom to deposit in my account, I had $65,000. I withdrew some of the money for Mom so she could go shopping for herself. Of course, I had to accompany her to the mall because otherwise she wouldn't buy anything. During the two years I was in the service, I would send half of my check home to Mom. She couldn't let on to WJ that I was doing this because he always had his hand out. Most of the money went into the bank with a small portion going to her for living expenses for her and J.J. Every so often she would give WJ a small piece of change to keep him out of her hair. Sometimes it didn't matter to me whether he got anything or not. At that time I didn't think it was a good idea to buy things for her because then WJ would assume she had money, which would make being in the house with him very tense for Mom. He had a habit of playing the big shot. Mom bought herself a few things here and there but food was always at the top of her list. Now that I was home I needed to find my own place to stay. There were some new apartments on Highway 80 West. I signed a lease for a three-bedroom apartment with a rent payment of $300.00 a month.

ULTIMATUM

After a week of job searching, I started driving the local school bus. I couldn't get a job in my field as a physician's assistant. My mother was still driving buses and working at the high school. WJ worked for the city. Thank God he had sense enough to at least work a 9 to 5. About a month after I was home, I secured a part time job at the same school that Mom worked at. One morning I was trying to talk to Mom, and she seemed to be avoiding me. I was really feeling bad by the third day because I had no idea what was wrong. At the time, I had a good baby sitter, which came in handy with my running around. I couldn't think of anything that I could have done to make her mad enough to want to avoid me. Had someone told her I was seeing two women at the same time? Did she know I was running from having to make a decision about living in Mississippi or moving to Florida to care for Kathy and Helen? I was torn between staying and leaving. In Florida, I owned a home and in Jackson I was renting an apartment. When my little brother came to the house that night, I told him how Mom was avoiding me. Maybe he could ease my mind and shed some light on the situation.

"James, Mom has a black eye that she is trying to hide from you. WJ hit her with the handle of his gun during one of his mad spells."

"What?" I began to block everything out. I had to stop and get a grip before my rage set in. I asked him to tell me everything and not to leave one single detail out.

"First let me inform you that Mom has to pay him to give her a ride to work. She even paid him to drive you to work before you bought your car."

"Okay tell me about the fight. What led to it?"

"It wasn't a fight! Daddy started drinking. He was visiting some of his friends or family's house. I'm not sure which. Mom said they were in the truck. He got mad about something, probably nothing knowing him. He grabbed the gun from under the seat and hit her with the handle. He didn't turn around to go home when he saw that her eye was swelling. They proceeded to their destination where he announced that 'this is what is done to whores when they don't do as he says." After hearing that story I wanted to see this bastard bleed. I got up then because I wanted to know where he was. My brother tried to stop me.

"James wait a minute. If you go out there now like this you are probably going to kill him."

"That's what I intend to do. I want that bastard dead for what he did to mom. The SOB should have been dead before my mom even thought of marrying him." I was pretty calm after a while but I had to make sure Mom was all right. This time she couldn't get away from me. I cornered her and pulled her hair back so I could see just how bad her eye was. She started crying.

"Please James. It's okay. It's not as bad as it looks. Tell me you don't have it in your mind to do anything to your father."

"Mom how can you ask me that after what he did to your face?" In my mind I wanted to kill him especially after hearing my mother defend him. I had been feeling that way for a long time but today I wanted to act on it.

Work couldn't have come at a better time because I needed to get away from her for a while because she was only making me angrier. In my mind I thought he had passed the stage of hitting his own wife years ago. I had never even thought about putting my hands on a woman. I'd rather walk away than do something that I would later regret. I wanted to scream. My boss came in the back door and took note of how I was acting.

"I am sorry Mrs. Jones but I get a little upset when I see my mother sporting black eyes at her age; I wouldn't want to see this happen to any woman at any age for that matter. It just makes me mad!!" I hit the wall and both people in the room jumped. I turned around and there was Mom standing in the doorway.

"Let me talk to you James."

"No. No. Mom you let me talk to you!   I haven't said anything for a long time. I sat back and watched while you worked like a dog. WJ sat on his butt and chased every woman that came his way. Why do you put up with his bull shit?"

"I stayed because I couldn't imagine starting over and having another man living with my children."

"No. I think you stay because you are afraid to leave and you keep hoping that he will change. You have been with the same man for 23 years. That's enough time to change the world. Wouldn't you say? Mom I hate to say this but you leave me no choice. God knows it's true when I say I hate WJ and I am beginning to feel the same way about you. I will never want a woman that will allow me to walk all over her. Mom I believe I speak for all of us when I say we all feel the same way about WJ. I have decided to move out of town. I didn't want to leave you but you just helped me make up my mind. I can't just sit around and watch him kill you or one of us while you say I shouldn't hold him accountable for it."

"James please don't leave. Give me the chance to leave WJ and try to get my life together."

"Let you leave?"

"Yes. Let me leave here first. Give me some time, at least until September 29, which is on a Friday. It is August now. It's only four weeks."

"I'll hold off but if you are not gone from this situation by September 30, I will leave and move to Florida." She sighed with relief. Despite giving my mother this ultimatum, I still had to make a choice about moving to Florida. I decided to give it some thought while the right decision will make it self-known. My mother would tell me to pray on it. Those were always her next words after I stated a problem.

That night I felt better but the thought had not left my mind about hurting WJ. He needed a taste of his own medicine. I could hear Mom say that God will fix it. Did he not say that he gave us five senses and that we should use them? After work, I picked J.J. up and went home to fix him dinner. Later that night, I gave him a bath and the little guy was so tired he went right to sleep. I had some time to think. The more I thought about it, I knew it would be a good move.

SOJOURN

I decided to call Florida. I enjoyed talking to Kathy and Helen.

"I will be down there this weekend." I knew it was short notice but I had to get away.

"Is J.J. coming with you? Oh James, I can't wait to see you and my great grandson." I just had to get away for a while so I decided I would leave the next day right after work. While warming up the bus, I told Mom that J.J. and I would be going out of town for the weekend.

"Where are you going? To Florida?"

"Yes. I have to check on the house because the tenants that I am renting to are talking about moving. I can kill two birds with one stone meaning J.J. could visit with Helen and Kathy while I take care of my business with the house. You never know I might need to live there one day." I know Kathy will spoil J.J. all over again. It had been eight months since I had been to Florida but I kept in constant contact with them by calling almost every weekend. No one but my sister knew Helen had been here on three separate occasions for a few days. Liz was always nice enough to keep J.J. while I took care of my business.

Friday after work I picked up J.J. and Mom so she could drop me off in Rankin County at the airport. She would have the opportunity to drive my car since the other kids were constantly using her old one. In the back of my mind I was a little worried about her. Everyday she was packing her stuff a little at a time while WJ was being too nice. I needed to get away from Mississippi because every time I looked at that bruise that my mother was trying so very hard to hide, my thoughts went right back to killing him over and over again. We got to the airport about an hour before take off time. I had a little time to relax and play with my son. My priority on this trip was to think about what I was going to do. I was lost in thought after I boarded the plane and got J.J. settled. While sitting there I saw a young lady who caught my attention with the warmest eyes and a smile that would stop traffic.

"It can't be that bad!"

"What?"

"Whatever you're thinking about? Excuse me I don't think you have noticed that your son has moved over four seats." I looked at J.J. and sure enough he had moved over four seats.

"Oh."

"Hi my name is Cassandra. Your son introduced himself. You're James?" Boy did I like the way she said my name. Talk about a good distraction to pull me away from my thoughts.

"Yes. That's correct. Thank you for keeping my son occupied but he wouldn't have gotten very far." I showed her the attachment around J.J.'s arm and me. Mom bought it for me to protect J.J. when we're in public. At first I thought it was a leash and we both laughed about that. "This is our first trip together since I returned home from the service." I didn't want her to think I had been in jail. Every time a black man indicates he had been away people automatically assume that away refers to prison.

"Where were you stationed?"

"In Vietnam for one year and Germany the next."

"I'm surprised you didn't come back married."

"No I went in for an education so that I would get a good job to be able to support me and my son."

"Where's J.J.'s mother?"

"She lives in New York. I get an occasional phone call from her but he doesn't really know anything about her. When he gets older I will have an answer for him that he can live with." There was a last call for our flight, which meant I would soon be in Florida.

"Here is my number. Why don't you call me sometime if you are ever in Chicago? Okay. See you around." This was J.J.'s first flight. He wanted to sit by the window and talk to everybody. The kid is friendly with every stranger. It was all I could do to keep him in his seat. I was afraid someone would walk off with him. There was a man sitting across the aisle who wanted to talk. I don't know why all the lonely people find me. I guess it was my smile or maybe my positive vibe. Jack once said I could smile and automatically make a person feel better.

"Hi. I have two children, a boy who is six years old and a girl who is four years old. I only get to see them one weekend out of each month and all holidays. How did you get so lucky?"

"His mother wanted a career and I wanted my child. She has never seen him; not even the day he was born. Her mother wanted her to have an abortion but I made her an offer she couldn't resist. She also got $30,000 of his great grandfather's money. So far we both have kept up our ends of the bargain." He looked so sad.

"I wish I had it like that. You just don't know how lucky you are buddy. My ex has a friend and they are talking about marriage. He wants to adopt my kids.

She wants me out of the picture but I love my kids and I will not give up without a fight." We talked a little while longer. Time seems to fly by when you're having a good conversation. By the time we landed, J.J. was asleep. Helen and Kathy were there on time to pick us up. I was really glad to see Helen. It had only been 2 months but that was a long time when you're talking about a woman you care for. I love women especially the way they look, smell, and taste. Helen was a perfect fit for all of these categories. The girl turned me on so much in two days that I could only imagine what might happen in a month or week's time. Mrs. Searight caught J.J. by the hand as we walked through the airport and all eyes were on us. It was clear that Helen and I were black, but it was hard to tell with J.J. because his hair was just as red as mine and curly. Not only that his eyes were a light green color. He could have passed for anything with a tan. There was no doubt that Kathy was white.

"James, I really missed you. Phone calls are nice but nothing beats spending time together." I suggested that we have dinner and go to the movies. I don't remember what was playing but dinner was something to remember. I love seafood so much that I can eat shrimp forever. I was feeling pretty good sitting here holding Helen's hand. I would do anything just so this moment would never end.

"I should call to make sure J.J. & Kathy are okay and then we can have a nice night cap."

"That would be nice. I know a place that would be perfect. I'll drive." J.J. reported that he and Kathy were playing cards and he was having a lot of fun. I told him that bedtime was near and that he could not stay up all night. Helen drove to the Best Western. It was a beautiful hotel that required her to make reservations two days in advance. We weren't in the room a good ten minutes before we were all over each other. I am not sure who threw in the towel first but I did realize just how much I needed her. She knew just how to satisfy me. I wanted to pay for the room but she wouldn't here of it.

"Not tonight. This one is on me. Next time when we're in Jackson you can pick up the tab." Helen was a good woman in that money didn't excite her, which is why I didn't mind buying her gifts every now and then. Helen had been in Jackson three times in the last 8 months. I took off work and she told Kathy that she had business to take care of in Memphis. We got a room at the Howard Johnson for one night and it was 24 hours of pure joy. I did things with Helen that I hadn't done with any other woman. I learned what a woman really tastes like while I was with Helen. We would make love for hours at a time. Kathy and J.J. were asleep when we got home which was around 12:45 a.m. We didn't plan on getting in so early but it wouldn't look good to J.J. if he saw us come in the following morning.

On Saturday, we went to Sea World with J.J. He loved it but I couldn't do anything with him because Kathy was having a ball with him. She wasn't about to let go of him for anyone. I couldn't believe that a woman her age could keep up with him. The five-year-old almost knocked the wind out of me. Kathy was only 50 years old although she didn't look a day over 35. We had such a good time that we really didn't want to leave. I just wanted to get back and take a bath because I was ready for sleep. We got back to the house around 6:00 p.m. Kathy and J.J. went straight to bed. I crashed on the sofa and I saw Helen go to her room. I woke up at about 1:30 a.m. thinking it was another day. Helen was up at the same time claiming she couldn't sleep. J.J. and Kathy couldn't sleep either so we all started laughing as if there was no tomorrow. Everybody was hungry so Helen made us all bacon and eggs. After we ate and sat around watching old movies, we all went back to bed hoping to sleep through the night. The clock read 4:00 a.m. I didn't have any problems falling asleep. We were all up around 10:00 a.m. "James, I want to go out to Fairmont to see Annie today. Would you and J.J. come with us?" I said yes rather quickly. I didn't want her to hear the hesitation in my voice. "She is making good progress. She knows Helen and me. I can tell that she really misses Jack.

It might do her good to see you and J.J. I'm sure she will remember you. We got dressed.

J.J. was clean with his three-piece suit and yellow shirt. He was stepping out in style. We all laughed at the way he was walking. As usual Kathy held his hand. The trip took about 45 minutes. It was a very nice day and the home resembled a resort center. It didn't really look like a care center it was so clean. "Annie has been here for two and ½ years. She seemed to have lost it after Jack died. She is now 24-25 years old. She is three years older than you James. Do you remember the way she would follow you around?"

"Yes. She would work right along with me." It was true. It just seemed as if autistic people would take to me. Even now on the job driving the school bus, when I get the special education group to take swimming and to the movies, they all wanted me to join them whether they were boys or girls, black or white, old or young. My thoughts were interrupted when Kathy called my name.

"James. Earth to James." My thoughts were definitely elsewhere. We had to go to the office to get permission to enter Annie's room. There were very few blacks there but at least we were present. We went down a long hallway with very neat rooms on each side. We came to Annie's room, which was very nice. It had a lot of dolls, books, and pictures. There was a picture of Jack and me taken at the store, one of J.J., Kathy, and Helen.

"When was this taken?" I asked. There was a picture on the wall that had been made by Kathy that was joined but had actually been taken in two different places I was told. Annie was so glad to see me. She hugged me for the longest time before she went to J.J. He was hugging her and to my surprise he acted as if he knew her. J.J. kept referring to her as Auntie Annie. Auntie Annie? I was a little puzzled. Okay. What is going on here? Before I could voice my thoughts Kathy decided to come clean.

OPPORTUNITY KNOCKS

"James, I think its time for me to come clean. I asked Ida to allow Liz to bring J.J. down here a few times while you were away. She did it only because I asked her to. Please don't be upset with your mother or me. You know that we are and always have been very close." I couldn't believe it. There were more damn secrets. When the hell does it end?

"So that's what Mom was not telling me the first time I came here. J.J. had been here before and Kathy knew everything about Jack and his family tree? I am glad that I never lied to her. I just didn't answer some of the questions that she asked. My mother could find a million dollars and never say a word about it to anyone. I guess that's where I get it from."

"When I took him to see Annie, she made so much progress that the doctor wanted me to bring him consistently to help her continue to progress. We thought it would be a good idea that he stays a while. The doctor came in and Annie was talking and playing with J.J. I couldn't believe it but they were actually communicating with each other as if she really knew she was his aunt. She walked over to me and started talking to me.

"J.J. is cute, He is so cute and I am glad to be his auntie."

"Yes, you are his auntie." I had to fight back the tears that were welling up in my eyes. I wouldn't have believed J.J. could improve her condition with a few visits if I weren't seeing it with my own eyes. Just think what progress she could make if J.J. came to see her once or twice a week. While I was lost in thought the doctor was talking to Kathy. I knew what was coming next. That explains why Kathy was so intent on me moving to Florida.

"James this is Dr. Waters. Dr. John Waters."

"Dr. Waters, this is James, J.J.'s father.

"I am afraid I have you at a disadvantage. I know all about you. How are you Mr. Bradshaw? Annie talks about you and J.J. all the time."

"Dr. Waters, are you trying to tell me that there is a chance Annie can recover just by being around my son?"

"Yes I am. From the first time your grandmother brought him out here something happened that medical technology couldn't explain. Mr. Bradshaw I want to offer you a job in physical therapy. I know this is something you want to think about. The pay is very good. Your mother mentioned your occupation as a physician's assistant in the service. There's just one more thing I want to add. As long as I am supervising over this center you won't have anything to worry about. If I get fired we both have to look for a new job." He laughed. I had to smile behind that because it was rare to see a doctor with a sense of humor.

"How can you have this kind of faith in me. You don't even know me."

"No but I know your grandmother and Annie. The rest is history." He was giving me direct eye contact, a quality I really admire in any person.

"Dr. Waters."

"Call me John."

"My field is really in dialysis. I was planning on moving to Chicago. I have a good friend working at Mount Sinai Hospital and one working at Michael Reese Hospital. They really want to get me started there. I am very good at inserting catheters, grafts, and fistula."

"James, you have an education and you are a trained physician's assistant. The only thing you need besides those two is on the job training. Your credentials would be kept confidential. We have a very good continuing education program. You could have your Associates in Applied Science in a year and a Bachelor of Science in two years taking classes right here in your spare time." I am standing there looking at this white doctor offering a 22-year old black man a job that I am not qualified for on paper. I don't doubt myself. I know I can do the job with a little training. I looked over at Kathy and Helen. They both dropped their heads but not before I could see the 'please say yes' in their eyes. "James, I know you have to return to Jackson tonight but can you come back next week? The hospital will pay for everything."

"Okay. I can be here next Saturday."

"Would it be possible for you to arrive at the hospital at 9:00 a.m."

"Sure." We walked over to join the others. Annie and J.J. were having a ball all over the place. I had a feeling and was almost sure that Helen and Kathy had overheard everything. We stayed about a half-hour longer and then visiting hours was over. Annie didn't want to say good-bye to any of us.

On the drive back everyone was happy while I had a lot of thinking to do. This would be a major move for me. Then there was my mother to consider. I could kill two birds with one stone. Maybe I could get my mother interested in moving to Florida. After all it was not far from Mississippi in case she wanted to return. Mom could out drive any man, so this would only be a hop, skip, and a jump for her. In addition she wasn't afraid to travel alone if she had to. I looked back at Kathy and found that she was sleeping peacefully. Why did my mind lead me to believe that she had a smile on her face?

MISSISSIPPI OR FLORIDA?

After we pulled into the driveway everyone got out. J.J. was asleep so I took him in myself. I got all the junk out of the car and washed the car for them. I just wanted to be alone and think. I really needed to be alone to get my thoughts together. After I finished I went inside and Helen had my bags packed for me. Kathy asked if Helen could take me to the airport. I said yes. She said good-bye without any mention of the upcoming weekend and my decision. Helen did the same. We talked about anything and everything except the hospital or Dr. Waters. We arrived at the airport at about 8:00 p.m. We both kissed her. I asked her not to wait around. J.J. was so quiet that I was a little worried about him.

"Daddy are we going to move to Florida?" I smiled.

"Why do you ask?"

"Auntie Annie said she wishes we could so I could come see her every weekend." I didn't answer. After boarding the plane, I strapped J.J. in and I went to sleep. The stewardess woke me up.

"Mr. Bradshaw, we will land in 10 minutes." J.J. was smiling and looking out the window.

"Daddy, Daddy, look at all the lights." It was 9:10 p.m. I wasn't worried about getting home because either Mom or Liz would be there to pick us up.

After claiming my bags, I had J.J. in one arm and the bags in the other. Mom and Liz were both there to meet us.

"Hi, did you guys have fun?" J.J. ran to Granny and gave her a big kiss.

"Granny, we might move to Florida."

"What!"

"Uh huh. Auntie Annie wants us to move down there with her." It's amazing how a youngster can take a few words and just run with it.

"Mann, what is J.J. trying to tell me?"

"Oh not much. I just got a job offer at the hospital that takes care of Annie. She is making so much progress every time she sees J.J. But you already know about that, right mother?" She looked down and smiled.

"Oh James don't be upset. No harm was done. Liz took J.J. to see Kathy a few times. I am sorry. I just didn't want to worry you while you were away in the service. So what are you going to do?"

"I don't know. I have a week to think about it. I'm supposed to go back next Saturday and give him my answer. After I get everything together and if I decide to move there, I will give a two week notice to both jobs."

"Well if it will help you to make up your mind, we could send Liz down to look for a place for me that is if you don't mind having your Mom around." I couldn't believe what I heard. I picked her up and kissed her. I'm going to get my house back in six months when the current tenant's lease expired.

"Mom you mean you would move to Florida with me?"

"No son. Not with you but before you." She smiled. The only thing standing in the way is making sure that no one knows where I am moving to. Her whereabouts certainly won't fall off my tongue. I made up my mind then and there. I was moving to Florida. I had only good dreams that night just knowing mom was leaving WJ. The next day I gave a 3 months notice to both jobs. After work I called John Waters. I told him I would keep the appointment for the weekend but I couldn't start work until December 1st. He said that was great.

"I will mail you the paper work before you change your mind."

"Oh. I won't change my mind." I sailed through the next day. I went to the bank and withdrew $1500 for Liz to travel to Florida to look for a place for Mom. She was off on her mission and WJ was lead to believe Liz went to Chicago to see a friend on business. Mom was packing little by little and storing it at my place. I didn't want anything to go wrong. Things were going as we planned and on schedule. That Friday after work, J.J. and me left for Florida. Helen picked us up at the airport at 8:30 p.m. Kathy was fixing a late snack when we arrived at her house.

"James. Hi J.J. My, honey is you hungry?"

"Kathy. J.J. is always hungry."

"I am a growing boy grandma." Everybody laughed. We sat around, watched TV, and talked. By 10:30 p.m. or 11:00 p.m. everybody was in bed. It had been a long day. Helen picked up on it. I really had a lot on my mind, so I wasn't in the mood for anything but rest and relaxation.

I arrived at Fairmont at 9:00 a.m. sharp. John Waters was there with his hand out. I shook it and said hello.

"I bought the papers with me and they are all signed."

"James, I am so happy that you decided to join my team. Annie has been asking for you."

"I will go talk to her now." As soon as I got to her room Annie ran straight to me.

"James. I knew you would come back. Where is J.J.?"

"He will be here later on. Visiting hours is not until 1:00 p.m. Don't worry he will be here." We toured the grounds with Annie holding my hand. Some looked pleased, while others looked puzzled. Dr. Waters was there to answer any questions anyone had about me. At about 11:00 a.m., I was starving.

We went to the lunchroom and I was really impressed with it. The food was great unlike most hospital and care center cafeterias that serve the worst food. I met a lot of young ladies that were willing to give me their phone number but I told myself to take things very slow. I could hear Papa Joe telling me never ever get your honey and money in the same place. It can turn into a huge problem. By the time we finished talking it was 12:45 p.m. Helen and Kathy had arrived. J.J. went with Annie. This gave me the opportunity to spend some time with Helen. I wanted everyone to know she was my lady. From some of the looks I got, I know I made my point but there were others that didn't really give a damn. Dr. Waters had to leave so I was free after 2:00 p.m. Helen and I were walking when her thoughts began to flow.

"Did you get your point across to the young ladies?" I laughed.

"You know me all too well."

"Oh. I don't mind. I love the idea of being a couple with you." At about 5:30 p.m. J.J. had fallen asleep and Kathy was tired. Annie was ready to eat and get back to her room. She didn't object when we left. Forty-five minutes is a long time to drive when you are sleepy. That night at about 12:30 a.m., Helen came to my room. This time I wasn't tired at all. If I was, my body didn't know it.

I was up at about 8:30 a.m. I went running. Helen told me Liz had called and she found a very nice two flat building. One apartment was a three bedroom and the other one was a two bedroom.

"That's great Liz." I knew I had to have my own place soon. I realize that I can't live with any one for too long. Liz had been in Florida for about a week. I believed the place would be nice. She wasn't the type to settle for less. Now that that was out of the way, she had more time to spend with her boyfriend. Liz had a man in almost every city. It was clear Liz was more like WJ. She said that's why she would never marry. It was just that there are too many men out there so why settle for just one? My sister was definitely the wild one. I told Kathy about my moving on December 1st. I knew Mom had filled her in already. I overheard them on the phone. They were probably comparing notes. I made arrangements to be on a 3:30 p.m. flight so I could get back to Jackson early. Helen dropped us off at the airport. Mom picked us up when we arrived in Jackson. Time went by so slow for the next two weeks. My mind was in over drive and I was sitting on pins and needles.

YOU DON'T MISS YOUR WATER UNTIL YOUR WELL GOES DRY

Today is September 25. I was thinking 5 more days and Mom will be far away from WJ. I talked to Mom at work. She had her keys to her apartment and her rental car, which was a Lincoln. She was ready to go. She loved the Lincoln cars so why not make sure she is satisfied? When I got there I could tell something was on her mind.

"What's wrong? Have you changed your mind?"

"No, no. Never."

"Well what's wrong? I know something is wrong because I can see it in your eyes." I knew she could hear the bitterness in my voice.

"Mann take it easy. Don't get so upset. Boy, you act as if you are a ticking time bomb which is why I am almost afraid to tell you anything."

"Mom, I am sorry. I am a little on edge but you can tell me anything now that I know you will be out of here in five more days." We both laughed. "Now what has got your mind so occupied?"

"Your daddy brought some of his women's clothes to Mae and me. I guess he thinks we need them. I can't wait to get away from here so I can shop without having to explain where I got the money. As hard as I work, I shouldn't have to explain anything to anyone."

"Why don't you take the clothes and hang them where you always hang yours and that way it will look as if things are still normal."

"That's a good idea baby."

"Mom when you get to Florida I am going to make sure you shop until you drop." My mother was afraid to spend money. WJ would always come home without a cent to his name. She was afraid she would need something for the kids or on a rainy day as she called it. I wanted to tell her I was more than prepared for a rainy day but I will wait. The only thing is my mother didn't know about my finances unless Kathy told her. I didn't tell her so she wouldn't be lying when WJ asked if she knew anything. She would truly be able to say she didn't know. Wednesday night I called Mom only to find WJ home. I was startled at him being home. The streets are his favorite pass time.

"What's up?"

"I had a little cold so I came home to rest." My thinking was he came home so Mom could wait on him hand and foot. His days are numbered though.

"How bad is the cold? Do you have a fever?"

"I don't know. Your mama is taking my temperature now." He was silent as Mom picked up the phone.

"Hi baby."

"Mom I know you can't talk but everything is going as planned. I'll call you tomorrow when you can talk. Okay. I love you." I didn't wait for an answer. I hung up. Liz was home for the first time in days. She had moved in about three months ago but was never home. She watched J.J. while I took a bath. Liz went out later on that night. I had to make a few phone calls. J.J. must have sensed that I was about to take care of some business.

"Daddy, can I take a bath?" I learned a long time ago not to leave J.J. in the bathtub alone. On one occasion I was giving him a bath when the phone rang. Granny and Papa Joe were both out. J.J. was about a year old. I left him to answer the phone. That was when he stood up and fell backward into the water. I heard a noise and when I ran into the bathroom J.J. was in the bathtub fighting for his life. I must have walked around with him in my arms while I cried and kissed him all over. I thanked God for sparing my son. I told Mom two weeks later but I never shared that with granny. So even now with him being 5 years old, he never takes a bath alone even though Mom and Liz had him take swimming lessons while I was in the service. He is like a fish in the water but that memory hasn't gone away.

Everybody else seems to be leaving with Mom. Left was Essie who was married to a man who was three times her age but he was very good to her. Everything was going as planned. Mom had gotten the last of her clothes out of the house. We were all surprised when Bobby, my brother, said he was going to stay around so it would be enough room in the car for everyone else. Peter was in the navy so Mom would only have to worry about John, Mae, RB, and Joy. We all knew Bobby always had a soft spot in his heart for WJ. He felt sorry for him for some reason that I just couldn't understand.

It was D-Day. Mom called me early Friday morning and said WJ wasn't going to work but that was okay too. She could still get a head start. He would assume she had a charter with the school. At 8:30 a.m., Liz took the car to Mom's job. Mrs. Jones and all the ladies that worked with her were so happy; it was as if she had won a sweepstakes. They all knew what kind of man WJ was. He had made a pass at all her friends, all the black ones anyway. He was afraid of Mrs. Jones's man. The showdown came at 2:30 p.m. when Mom took the bus in. Liz drove the car to the bus depot. Mom loaded everything up and was on her way. I gave her $1000 in cash. She wouldn't take any more than that. As I watched them drive away I saw that Mom was leaving WJ for good. All the siblings were happy. I felt a little sorry for him. I felt a little remorse for him but not enough to spare his feelings. At about 6:30 p.m. my phone rang.

"James have you seen Mom since work?" It was Bobby. I knew WJ was looking right into his mouth.

"Not since about one or two when I took a load of kids to the zoo from the bus depot. Maybe she had a charter today." I was lying my butt off because I could hear WJ in the background.

"Okay." He was all right with this answer and hung up the phone. The guy should have been in Hollywood because he had missed his calling. He could keep a straight face in any situation. I was clowning on the other end and not once did he let on.

At about 7:30 p.m. WJ and Bobby were at my front door.

"Those were not her clothes hanging up in the closet." I was the first to speak. Liz was in the bedroom on her knees. She was laughing so hard that Bobby closed the door on her so she wouldn't give us away.

"She is gone. She's gone Mann."

"What did you do to her this time? Did you hit her with the gun again?" He stopped and looked at me as if I had shot him.

"James, I was…I told her I was sorry. I am sorry. I am sorry." I was mad as hell by this time.

"You are sorry. You are one sorry motherfucker. If it had been left up to me she would have been gone 15 years ago." Essie and Bobby were pulling me inside.

"Come on James man. Give the old guy a brake. Mom's gone now. He can't hurt her anymore."

"Yes, you're right. Ha! Ha!"

"Mann do you know where she went? I just need to talk to her one last time. I can change. I will. I can change."

"It's a little to too late for that." We knew mom wasn't the kind of person that listened to other people because once she made up her mind about something that was it. It took her 23 years to leave. He knew it would take another 23 years for her to think about returning to him. He was crying and begging at this point. "Tell me where she is. I just need to talk to her for just 5 minutes."

I didn't say anything. I just walked away. All I could see was years of abuse in my mother's eyes four weeks ago. My mother endured years of heartache. She married him at 16, had me at 17 and on and on and on it went until she had 10 children. She just jumped from the skillet into the fire. Essie left with her family and Bobby took WJ home. I went inside and thanked God for getting my mother out of this mess. Only Essie, Peter, Liz, Bobby, and me really know what she went through with WJ. He did everything short of bringing his women home with him. Most people that didn't know him probably thought he was a single man.

I was up the next morning around 4:30 a.m. I didn't sleep very well. I was waiting for a phone call from Mom. She left Jackson around 3:00 p.m. (this was 4:00 p.m. E.S.T.) I made coffee, then I saw that Liz was up too. I asked her, "can't you sleep?"

"No. We should hear something from Mom soon? Right?" By 6:00 a.m. the phone rang. We only hoped that it would be Mom.

"Hi baby. It's Mom. We're here."

"Did you drive all night?"

"Yes! I rested for 2 hours then started again."

"Where are you?"

"I am at Kathy's. Helen is going to take us to the apartment after breakfast."

"Okay. That's great. Tell everyone I said hi."

"Oh wait. Wait." She made me speak to everyone. Helen was the last one I talked to.

"I can't wait to see you."

"Me too." That was all I could say. I couldn't believe Mom had finally left WJ. She really did it!!! As if reading each other's minds Liz and I both started laughing and jumping around. We made so much noise that we woke J.J. up. He came running into the room.

"Daddy what's wrong?"

"Oh auntie and Daddy are just happy." We were careful not to mention Mom to him right then because WJ loved J.J. There was no doubt in my mind about that. I know J.J. would have told him about Mom just as soon as he saw him. He would say 'grandma call grandpa.' An innocent child not knowing what was going on would more than likely say the wrong thing. The phone rang again at about 7:00 a.m. It was WJ.

"Mann I know you know something. Where is your mother?"

"What makes you think I know where she is?"

"Because you are not worried about her, and I know how close you two are."

"I was worried all night, but I also know that no news is good news and bad news travel fast. I know that wherever she is, she is okay."

"James if you knew where she was would you tell me?"

"No!"

"Okay." I understood at that very moment that he knew I was going to tell him the truth. I tried to tell the truth all the time. Sometimes it was hard dealing with the ladies though. Some make it seem as though you have to lie to them or you weren't a real man.

Mom had been gone a week today. WJ looked as if he had aged 10 years in one week. He used to take pride in his physical appearance but now he didn't seem to care as much. I know he had two women besides my mother but now he was not interested in seeing either of them. I tried to talk to him but all he would say is I want your mom back. I asked him did it take her leaving for him to love her. He just said you never really know what you have until you lose it. He knew deep down inside that she would never return to him and so did I. My mother wasn't a person to jump into anything nor did she take advice from other women. I can honestly say Kathy was the only real friend I had ever known her to have that was worth talking about. Her life mostly centered on work, church, her children, and Granny when she was living.

WJ looked so bad I felt sorry for him but there was nothing I could do. Granny used to say when you make your bed hard you just have to lie in it. God knows his bed was made of rocks right now. He would come by just to see J.J. They were crazy about each other despite his reputation with everyone else. It took me two months before I had the heart to tell him I was leaving. By that time he had talked to Mom but it didn't do him any good. She was out of his life permanently. It was clear that the kids could see him any time they wanted to but Mom was off limits. I know that after I leave town I won't see him again. The pain was very much evident in his eyes when I said I was leaving November 23rd so that I would have time for my birthday. I would be starting my new job on December 1st. WJ's world was crumbling down around him and there was nothing he could do about it. A water picture goes to the well a long time and it finally come up broke. Mom took all she could for 24 years, which is a very long time to be mistreated by someone that claims to love you. WJ came around but not as much after that conversation. It was easy to say good-bye to my ladies. One was married and the other was engaged to be married. I didn't want any strings attached. I knew someday that I would be leaving Mississippi. It was just a matter of time and the right opportunity coming along. Karen said she understood and if we could spend just one more night together it would be great. I didn't make any promises. That's what I liked about her. She didn't expect anything from me but my time. I did buy her a few gifts during our affair. Alice was just the opposite. Even though she was engaged she wanted me. I was cautious with our relationship by keeping it a friendship-lover thing because I knew the day would come when I would leave the state of Mississippi for good only returning to visit. After arriving home, I called Mom again just to talk. I made it a point not to talk about WJ.

A NEW BEGINNING

November 23rd was finally here. I was excited as I loaded the U-Haul. I was driving and Liz was taking the ride with me. It didn't take but 10 hours to drive to Florida. I went straight to Mom's house, got unpacked and called Helen and Kathy. They arrived before I could get my clothes back on. I called WJ and Bobby just to let them know that I had made it safely. He was a real ass hole as a husband and father but now he was a lonely 44-year old man that looked as if he had aged 20 years in two months. I wanted to get on with my life and now is my chance. We sat around talking. Tomorrow I would get furniture for my new place. Liz agreed to live with me until I got my house. Then she would keep the apartment.

We all sat around talking. I was looking at Mom. I saw a glow in her eyes that I hadn't seen in years. Looking closely I realized it was freedom that contributed to her glow. This was something that she never had much of before. My mother was finally free to do as she pleases. She was on her own. I sensed a little fear *also* but she had us, and I could afford to take care of her if necessary. One day I would sit her down and explain to her just how much money I really did have. Kathy and Mom were chatting nonstop. They were making plans for church on Sunday. My mother belonged to a mixed church. She had said before, "Mann its every nationality you can think of and everyone gets along like one big family."

I wasn't tired of hearing her talk but my body was tired from the trip. I had to lie down for a while before I fell down. I went and took a nap in Mama's bed, which is something I haven't done in years. I slept like a baby. When I woke up everybody was eating so naturally I joined in. I got ready to go shopping because I needed to get furniture for my new place. There was so much love in the house that I hated to leave even for a few hours. I have to admit that every now and then WJ would cross my mind and I missed Bobby too. I saw a nice bedroom set for myself but didn't get it. I really didn't know how to work this. Liz made plans to stay with me. I only had two bedrooms. I couldn't put J.J. in the room with her so I decided to get twin beds for my room. I wasn't planning on female company anyway at least not at home. I got a nice full size set for her room. I didn't have a problem bunking with J.J. My house had three bedrooms. I wrote Mrs. Rogers, the current tenant, and gave her six months notice. She was a nice lady that understood that I would need my house. She would be out by May of next year.

I got my place furnished rather quickly. I must admit it looked very nice with Liz and Helen's help. I called Bobby and gave him my phone number. We talked for quite a while. I said hello to WJ and then J.J. talked to him. The weekend went well although I didn't get much rest between trying to pay attention to Mom and Helen.

I was introduced to everyone three months ago so I just fell right into my work. I really loved my job. J.J. loved his new school and my mother was happy with the way things were going for her. What more could I ask for? Dr. Waters were awaiting my arrival. I had a good shift, which started at 8:00 a.m. and ended at 4:00 p.m. with some overtime. The patients generally didn't start coming in for physical therapy until 8:30

in the morning and were out by 3:00 or 3:30 p.m. in the afternoon.

The first thing I tried to do was get mama to give up her job and allow me to pay her to keep J.J.. My mom said, "no." The woman didn't know anything but work. Kathy was just as bad because she had started volunteering at Fairmont just so she could see Annie on a daily basis.

About a month after I left Mississippi, Bobby and WJ had a falling out and Bobby decided to leave. It seemed as if WJ accused him of being on drugs. I couldn't understand that because WJ would give us reefer and a little something to drink. Of course I didn't tell Mom, but Liz knew about it. He had always tried to get me to party with him, but I always said, "no." Even before I left for the service, if I saw him in a bar, I made it my business not to go there. He was always trying to give me pot or a joint as he called it. I would always get away by saying no thank you to avoid hurting his feelings.

I learned my job very well. Annie seemed to be doing fine and the rest of my patients loved me. I learned a lot about sick people. They don't care about the color of your skin as long as you know what you are doing and you respect them; they will do the same in return.

I had planned on building a good relationship with Helen. She has been a little distant every since I moved here. Every time I try to get down to the root of the problem she would only say, "I want things between us to stay as they are. If you find someone else, go for it."

I accepted this for a while until we went away for a weekend. She couldn't run or change the subject then. She had to talk to me whether she liked it or not. "Helen, I want to know once and for all what the problem is?"

"James, you know you are 24 and I am 30."

"Don't give me that age shit again. Age is just a number. If I keep living I will be 30 in six years. I didn't mean to snap but I'm not interested in age." I was thinking of asking the woman to marry me some day. J.J. loves her and she gets along with my mom extremely well.

"James, we can't let this get any more serious than it already is. You see when I was a kid I got hit by a car. As a result of that accident, I can never have children and I know for a fact that you want more kids."

"We have talked about this before." We did talk about this long and hard but never did she say anything about not having kids. "So now that you have picked my brain you are going to use that against me?"

"Honey, don't be mad at me. I will always be here for you but I will not marry you nor will I make a commitment to you."

"Helen if I am involved with someone, I don't sleep around especially if we have something that I feel is going some place. What do you think, this is a game?"

"James, I just want you to find someone to make you happy." We left it at that. We were together a lot but never did we talk about commitment with each other again, nor did the word love come up. I got into my work, which I loved, took care of J.J., and tended to my patients. Everyone around me was pretty happy.

SUNSHINE MAKES AN APPEARANCE

I had been in Florida for two years. Dr. Water and I were working on a new project for some of the older patients' treatment. I told him I needed a break. I was walking down the hall when I saw her. Even a hundred feet away I knew this was Mrs. Right. She stood about 5'10"and weighed 150 or 160 lbs. God she had legs to die for and her skin looked like milk chocolate. I had a thing for brown, tall, big-legged women. I knew this was the future Mrs. Bradshaw.

As we approached each other our eyes met. I initiated the conversation. "Hello. Nice day isn't it?"

"Yes," she said in a voice that would melt sugar.

"Do you work here?" I asked.

"Yes and no. I work at the main office. A few of us come here for a late lunch sometime." I knew about the main office but never had any reason to go there. "This time no one showed up but me," she was saying.

"Well, I was just on my way to get a cup of coffee. Care if I join you? Oh, I am sorry. I am Bradshaw, James Bradshaw."

"I've heard so much about you. I am Rachel Walls and I would like that very much."

"I hope some of the things you've heard about me wasn't all bad."

"No, quite the contrary. I have to say it was very good."

"Well Rachel Walls, I am afraid you have me at a disadvantage. I don't know anything about you."

"Well there is not much to tell. My family moved here from Cleveland 10 years ago. My father is a doctor and my mother is deceased. I have a sister but she is married and lives in Cleveland, Ohio." We got coffee, a sandwich, and a table by a window for it was a very lovely day. She was a very beautiful woman to me. We talked more. I told her about J.J., my family, and my job. She worked in the Public Relations Department. She started working 2½ years ago and enjoyed her work very much.

We had been dating for three weeks. It didn't take long for everyone to pick up on it. I went shopping for new clothes. I dressed nice but I needed to up date my wardrobe, so I put my thoughts into action. I went all out by buying new socks, shoes, and ties. I was out of $3,000.00 for four out fits alone. Everyone said John and me dressed alike. I was too busy with work to worry about how I was dressed. Even John picked up on my new attitude. I just smiled and told him all about her.

"Well it looks like one of us will get lucky this year." We both laughed. John's wife left him. She said she couldn't compete with his work and the patients. "James if you have found Mrs. Right, please spend some time with her because money is not everything. They need you more so than your bank book, but some will actually settle for that." We laughed again. I left the office. I was going away with Rachel this weekend.

This was our first weekend away together so I asked Liz to keep J.J. for me. Mom would be at church Friday, Saturday, and Sunday night. He loved Grandma but he didn't want to go to church every night so Liz was going to keep him for me.

We took a cruise to the Bahamas. It took only 2 ½ hours to get there. Everyone kept referring to us as the newly wed couple. We did look good together even if I did say so myself.

We made reservations at the Marriott on Paradise Island. The sun was setting as we checked in. The scenery couldn't have been more beautiful if I had ordered it personally. After checking in, we were given a suite with a balcony. The suite was larger than my apartment. It was overlooking the ocean. The moon was full and bright as day. "We can go to dinner if you like," I said.

"No let's just get something cold to drink." I ordered room service. We had champagne, which I didn't too much care for but for her I would have drank anything including Crown Royal. I wasn't a drinker so I only had one glass. She really enjoyed it.

Rachel said, "I think I will slip into something more comfortable." While she changed, I got a quick shower. I had to clear my head and a shower always worked. We both walked back into the room at the same time. She was wearing pink. God she looked like an angel. Her hair was down. I wasn't used to seeing it this way because it was always in a twist and pinned to her head. She was wearing very little make up and looked 18 instead of 23. She walked right up and put her arms around my neck. We kissed for three minutes nonstop. I was so happy. I've been thinking about this all week. Her lips felt soft and warm. The way she moved her face back and forth, my mouth completely covered hers. Then we opened our mouths to explore each other. I could feel her tongue gliding over my teeth and licking the roof of my mouth as I kissed her back. Her tongue was sweet and hot all at once. We were writhing and twisting, trying to get closer to each other's sweetness. Each touch made her arch her back. I didn't fumble or grope. I knew just where my hands were supposed to be. I put my hands on her breasts, and she stopped breathing for a moment, a long time really.

Her breasts filled my hands. Moving my fingers back and forth *until* I could feel her nipples stiffening beneath her bra. I rubbed the back of my hands across her skin at the top of her cleavage. I felt her moving a little closer to me. I wanted to take my tongue and plunge it between her breasts.

"Baby" she was whispering into my ear. "You are so sweet, sweet, sweet." We walked to the bed.

I asked, "Are you ready for this? You can still change your mind. You are in the driver's seat." I know a nervous woman when I see one. She appeared to be a little nervous.

"No, I am fine." I began caressing the back of her neck and shoulders until I felt her going limp.

"Relax," I said. "Lie down." I removed her negligee. I bent down and kissed her face and neck. "You are so pretty." At this point I felt a little nervous. She pulled me down on top of her. The towel I had around me was on the floor. She was groaning, pulling me closer and calling me daddy.

"Daddy, please just take me now. I am on fire." She was not lying. We rocked each other's world all night long. She was really good in bed. The next morning I awoke at 7:00 a.m. with her sitting on top of me riding bare back. It didn't take us long to fulfill every need we both had. We took a bath together and made love again. This was heaven on earth. I never wanted it to end. By the time we got to breakfast, it was lunchtime. The hotel had a nourishing brunch buffet. I could have eaten a cow but Rachel just drank orange juice and ate toast. All through the day she would have something cold to drink but nothing much to eat. We had a great time. I bought souvenirs for everyone including Helen. I picked Helen, Mom, and Liz's gift myself. I felt these gifts should come from me. Rachel was in her own world. While shopping I could tell she was very materialistic and money meant a lot to her. Maybe it had something to do with the fact that she came from a family with a lot of it. We walked and shopped for hours. We were back in our room around 5:00 p.m. I wanted to go out for dinner, while she wanted room service. We had room service again. We sat and talked for hours. Communication was not a problem between us. We took a bath, stood on the balcony, and drank in the moonlight. We talked and she filled me in on her family. Rachel believed her mother committed suicide because her father was never home and he was having an affair with his nurse. She was eight years old when her mother died. She remembers a lot of shouting and crying coming from the bedroom. She said her father would never talk about it. I had met her father once and he seemed to be a very nice and warm man. I couldn't see him having an affair with anyone. He had some of the most honest eyes I had ever seen. I gave her some detail of my background which included Linda, Betty, my father, a little about Jack, Kathy, and very little about Helen or my financial status. She has met Mom and my family once. It was only brief and everyone was nice to her. I wanted to get off the sad stuff though, because this was a vacation for me in a way and I wanted to enjoy it. It didn't take long before we were back in the bed again.

The next day, which was Sunday, we got the opportunity to go out to lunch after dressing. Rachel was a knock out in her pink and gray dress. I knew pink was her favorite color. She loved it and was wearing it well. Entering the restaurant, all eyes were on us. I got quite a few winks myself which I returned with a smile. I have never really been a flirt but I knew I never had to go home alone. We ate in complete silence. We rented a car and went further inland. Upon arriving there we did more shopping. I had to buy another piece of luggage just to carry everything home. We had a fantastic time although I was a bit concerned about Rachel's eating habits.

Our ship was sailing at 4:30 p.m., which meant I could be home by 10:00 p.m. after dropping Rachel off. After all the shopping I asked again did she want something to eat. I was a little worried about her. She wasn't taking any kind of medication that I knew of. She couldn't be on a diet, at least not for me anyway. Her size and legs are what got my attention in the first place. When I mentioned her not eating she just smiled. "James if I get hungry I will eat. Don't worry I do eat. I think I probably caught some bug but I feel much better now."

After packing, I returned the car and got the shuttle bus to the dock. This time we were content on sitting in the dining area. After docking in Miami, I got my car and loaded everything up. Rachel was very tired so I took her straight home, kissed her good night, and said I would call her later in the week.

J.J. and Liz were up when I got home. I thought Liz was going to move after I moved into my house but she didn't. She just reminded me that I needed her more now than ever. I worked days and she worked nights so I always had someone to keep my son. J.J. ran and jumped into my arms. I almost fell and Liz cracked, "Are you a little weak James or just a little lighter?" We both laughed hoping J.J. didn't get it.

"I think I am a little of both."

"Yes. I could use a weekend like that myself."

"You won't get it if you don't get out and meet someone." We all knew Liz would take off to Jackson once or twice a month but she hadn't gone in the last three months. She didn't talk about it and I didn't ask. That's why we got along so well. We could talk about anything but we respected each other's privacy. She would tell me when the time was right.

"You know today was family Sunday and Mama cooked. She sent you some food."

"Good I will take it for lunch tomorrow."

"Yes. She thought you would so it's enough for John, too."

"You mean enough for me." We both knew that John loved Mom's cooking so well he would eat my lunch and buy me food from the cafeteria. I was used to it. I gave J.J. his gift, which was a camera. He loved it and couldn't wait to try it out. Liz got jewelry, which was what she expected. Every time I took a trip I bought her jewelry because she collected the stuff. Everyone got Liz jewelry from wherever they traveled. It was about 10:06 p.m., which meant that I had time to call Mom and Kathy. I had to because Kathy was worse than Mom over me and the rest of the family. We always tease each other about having a black mama and a white mama.

"Honey now you call me tomorrow and tell me all about your trip." I would because there were some things I could tell Kathy that I couldn't tell Mom. Mama dealt with the heart while Kathy dealt with the heart and the logical. When it came to money Kathy was my right hand girl. I guess it was because she had it and Mama didn't.

"Okay Mom. I'll call you tomorrow." She loved it when I called her Mom. When Mom was around I would play it off and say my two moms. Over all it worked and they were the best of friends and we all got along just like one big extended family. I took a shower and hit the sack. I was dog-tired. I have to remind myself to start back to exercising. This love making and walking had my body aching. My body was down right hurting. I had good dreams that night.

John couldn't wait for me to get in and get my coat off. He was all ears. Whoever said men don't gossip probably just didn't know any that did. We were worse then women when we got together. He did very little dating but he had a friend. I was shocked to find out that she was a mixed black and American Indian woman. I must say she looked homely and a bit bony, not my type at all.

"Oh we have a good lunch today. Mom cooked yesterday."

"Yes. I know. It was family day. I keep up with it too. Now stop pussy footing around and tell me every thing and don't leave anything out. How was she?"

"Oh. You mean the trip. It was great."

"James, man tell me about Rachel. I have been to the Bahamas. I know what it looks like."

"Man the girl is everything I hoped for and more. The only thing that bothers me about her is that she doesn't eat."

"Well look at it this way, you will save on food."

"Another thing that was unusual was that she never wanted to leave the room. I haven't had it like that since Helen was my honey."

"Boy. Helen looks like she could really make a man happy. She wouldn't give me the time of day."

"You tried?"

"Yes, before you met her. She wanted nothing to do with me. She was with Mrs. Searight all the time when they came to visit Annie."

"That reminds me, I have to call Kathy"

"Okay. You make your call but I want details and I do mean d-e-t-a-i-l-s." We both laughed. I called Kathy.

"Now how did she act?"

"Rachel was fine. We shopped and really had a good time."

"I know she is very materialistic."

"Kathy you have only met her once."

"I know but James if you know people you don't have to be around them forever to know them.

There are only two kinds of people, the givers and the takers. You are a giver and I believe she is a taker." I really didn't want to hear this, but I was cool because I knew she had my best interest at heart. One thing about Kathy was that she would speak her mind. After Jack's death, I think she realized that she was on her own. We talked a little while longer and I had to go.

"How about dinner one night this week?"

"Okay. Call me."

LIFE NEVER GOES WITHOUT DRAMA

Things were going very good. I was in love, or I was in love with the sex. I am not sure which. Things were going great at work and at home. The best thing was that no one was on my back about anything.

I was working late one night. I had a project that had to be done. I was winding up when Rachel walked in. Looking at her eyes, I knew something was wrong. We've been seeing each other two or three times a week for the last 4 weeks. "What's up?" I asked from sheer fear.

"James, I feel that it would be better if we don't see each other anymore." I wasn't sure I heard her right.

"What do you mean? What have I done? I know I work a lot but I always have time for us." I couldn't understand just what was going on. I wanted this woman in the worse way. "I know you are going to tell me why we can't see each other any more. Or is it just a request that has no reason?"

"James, I have a problem. I've thought about it and prayed about it. I just don't know what to do. My father said to let my conscious be my guide. I feel as if I am going to lose my mind."

"What is it? Can I help?"

"James, I am pregnant." I couldn't believe my ears. She didn't look pregnant or is there a look for pregnancy? I looked at her stomach. "I am only six weeks," after seeing the question in my eyes.

"Where is the father?"

"I don't know. It was a whirlwind romance. I thought we were in love. I was very careful, but shit happens."

"Did you know this before our trip? Is that why you weren't eating?"

"I didn't know I was pregnant. I just thought I had the flu. James, I am really sorry. I didn't mean to lead you on. I really do love you. I don't believe in abortion so that is out of the question. I don't know what to do but I don't feel I should drag you into my mess."

"Rachel then there is only one thing left to do. Have the baby. When I fell in love with you, I fell in love with anything that comes along with you." I remember Papa Joe saying if she has kids then she is a package deal. When you take her, you take the child as well. He said that marriage is for better or worse. When you make a commitment or agreement, it's not something you take back when you get mad or the person turn they're back on you, which sometimes happen. You live up to your end. A child is not a car. You can't give it back. It's for keeps. Kids get attached and their feelings are easily hurt.

I asked her to marry me and I agreed to take the child as my own. The subject of it not being mine would only come up if necessary like in a case of a medical emergency. This was a commitment we both made. Only her father and my mother would know the truth. I will tell them in my own time.

I told Mom and Liz first that I was getting married. They were happy for me but Liz voiced her real apprehension.

"I don't trust her."

Mama said, "If you can live with her then I can speak to her." That was all she said. Everyone else in the family would probably go along with our commitment to each other. The only issue was my other Mom, Kathy. In addition I had to tell Helen and Annie. Helen was very happy for me because this was exactly what she wanted. Kathy pulled me aside and made me promise not to let any woman know everything about my finances at least not right now anyway.

She went on to say, "Get to know her better first before you start trusting her. James even people that love you can change when it comes to money." She kissed me and said, "You are my son, and I want you and J.J. to be happy. I will kill someone before I see you hurt." Annie was very happy that she was going to be in the wedding.

J.J. and I talked about it and he was happy about Rachel, but deep down inside he would have been happier if it was Helen that I was marrying. He was crazy about her.

"J.J. you know Helen and me are just good friends and besides, she will always be a part of your life."

"Okay Daddy but can I stay at granny's or Kathy's for a while?"

"Why?"

"I just want to."

 By the weekend I was happy. Everyone knew I was getting married.

John said, "I hope she makes you very happy." His eyes were saying something else that I really couldn't put my finger on. You could only get out of John what he wanted you to know. "James she is lovely. I wish you the best." I could feel a but coming but I let it go and proceeded with the wedding.

WEDDING BELLS ARE RINGING

We set the date for the wedding. As a courtesy to Rachel, her father decided he wanted to pay for everything. Our colors were lavender and white. I talked her out of pink. Lavender was light enough for me. I wasn't about to wear pink because there is nothing masculine about it. Nerves took up most of our time before the wedding. She had a hard time deciding on her dress, the flowers, and the attendants. She was really worried about how she was going to look. She needed to be reassured over and over that everything was going to be fine. We both had second thoughts and lots of nervous attacks in the final days. Maybe it was best we did it so fast because there was less time to think about it. Our biggest concern was someone noticing or being able to tell she was pregnant. She wasn't showing, but old people had a way of being able to tell these things. We had a very small church ceremony. There were just two people present in addition to us. Afterward we went to a restaurant for dinner with immediate family. There were about 30 people present, mostly my family and some friends from my job. Her father and sister attended.

We didn't make a big deal about going on a honeymoon. Neither one of us were worried about it. Rachel wanted to go away, but I said that we could plan it for after the baby came. We left it at that.

THREE AND ½ MONTHS LATER…

"James." I looked up and saw it was Kathy. She looked like a woman with a lot on her mind. She was standing in the doorway of my office. This meant something was wrong because she never visited me in my office especially not in the middle of the day. She would call first.

"Mom, what's on your mind?"

"I was looking at Rachel yesterday during and after dinner." We had dinner with her and Mom the day before. "She is showing a lot to be only 3 ½ months pregnant. Are you sure she is only 3 or 4 months or is there something you're not telling me? She looks more like she's 5 or 6 months. Hun, you two didn't waste any time with this little bundle of joy."

"No, it's just that we are a couple of real speedy people." I smiled.

"James, I hope you didn't rush into this wedding just because she was pregnant. This is the eighties. It's no big deal to live together or have a baby out of wedlock." It sounded like my Mom and Kathy have been talking. They probably had a talk last night and agreed to put Kathy up to asking me these questions. This was a matter I really wasn't going to get into until I really had too. I would find a way to tell them about the baby one day. Right now all my energy went into the new unit. We opened up a new hemodialysis department about six months ago and it was my baby. I learned it during the service stage, and I must admit I was very good at it. I was an expert on catheters, grafts and fistula. I taught John everything he knows. Other doctors and nurse's and clinics were trying to recruit me to come and work for them, but I was happy with my present job and the salary wasn't bad either. John and I always discussed my different offers. We got a kick out of watching them try and convince me to leave my current job.

"Kathy I will talk to you later about this. I have too much on my mind right now. Maybe later my mind will be more at ease." She left.

THE TRUTH SHALL SET YOU FREE

Betty's big break came about six months after I got married. I got a phone call from Kathy first. "James turn your TV to Channel 7. It's Betty." She was performing. She was a very good entertainer so she worked hard to maintain her position. She would call sometimes just to say hello and ask about J.J. He knew her as Aunt Betty. He never asked how she was his aunt and I never said. I looked over at Rachel and she was smiling. "Your ex is good."

Rachel had all of Betty's records. I never really listened to her music because I could always hear something relating J.J. or me in the lyrics. I never really told Rachel much about Betty Moore. I only told her that she was my first love. For some reason she never asked for any more information until now.

"James just how close were you and Betty?" I looked deep into her eyes before I answered.

"We were about as close as two people could get. I was her first if you know what I mean." She dropped her eyes and she looked hurt. I wasn't about to tell her anything else about Betty's private life because from what I had read no one knew that she had a child with the exception of family members.

"James, where is J.J.'s mother?" This was a subject I wasn't ready for.

"She is around. I told you she lives in New York. You know she calls sometime. We have an agreement. I have full custody of J.J. She gave up all of her rights to him." My voice was changing and I could tell. Wanting to change the conversation I asked, "What's for dinner?"

"James why is it that you never talk about her? Why do you always change the subject?"

"I don't change the subject. You know I never talk about one woman to another. So let's just turn the page. That chapter is closed." She knew that was the end of it on this subject. Rachel went to get dinner started. I put my head back, closed my eyes and I relived my life with Betty. I would never admit it to myself but I was still in love with her in some way. There was a part of my heart that only she would have. No one else could get to it. That was the way I would keep it. I knew Kathy taped the show. I would get it from her and look at it one day.

During dinner Rachel made it a point not to mention the show again. We ate and I did the dinner dishes. Rachel went to bed. I knew I wasn't going to be able to sleep so I worked on a few notes for my job. I wanted to call Kathy, but I would wait until tomorrow. I didn't sleep very well. I was up at 6:00 a.m. and dressed shortly thereafter. I cooked and made a pot of coffee. Rachel got up later on and took a shower.

"James what's wrong? You didn't sleep much. I heard you tossing and turning all night."

"I have a lot on my mind with the job and the baby coming." Rachel was 8 ½ months pregnant. Everyone else thought she was 6 months. Mom made a comment that she noticed that her stomach had dropped. I said to myself that Mom is too smart for her own good.

I called the clinic and said I was going to be late. I called Kathy and told her to meet me at Mom's. I had to talk to both of them so why not kill two birds with one stone. I needed to get the truth about this baby thing out into the open. I wasn't good at living a lie. I didn't talk to Rachel about it because I felt this was up to me. I should have done this 7 months ago.

By the time I got there, Kathy was on her first cup of coffee. They were alone and Mom was waiting on the edge of her seat. "James is something wrong?"

"Mom, I just have to come clean with the two of you. It's about Rachel, the baby, and me." I told the entire story not leaving anything out. I even told them about last night and the way that I was feeling after seeing Betty's performance and the conversation with Rachel afterward.

"Rachel will need help in a few weeks and we will be there son. If you love and want this baby, then as far as I'm concerned it is our grandbaby." This was mom's response. I really loved that woman. She has always been there for me, always having something positive to say.

"James, I am just glad you are a part of my life. This did cross my mind but if you are happy, then I can live with any decision that you make."

"Thanks, Kathy." We were all in each other's arms kissing and crying. Now that, that was out in the open I felt as if I could finally get on with my life and live in peace.

WHAT GOES AROUND COMES AROUND

A few days later we got the word that WJ was really sick. Liz and Bobby rushed there to see about him. I left for Mississippi the following day but he was dead by the time I arrived in Jackson. I had called him a few times in the past. I even went back to Jackson but everything was the same. He looked really old the last time I saw him. I remember him telling me he would do anything to get Mom back but even he knew that would never happen. I felt sorry for him. He said to me once, 'If you get a good woman, be good to her, stay home with her and for God's sake don't listen to your friends. They are more than likely jealous. They want what you have. They will give you all this advice but when your woman leaves you they all leave too knowing they have been successful in making you miserable. You will be all alone. At that point, you will find out who your real friends are. James, I am happy you took after your mother and didn't inherit all of my ways.' That was the first and last father and son talk that WJ and I really had. Every other encounter was a brief hello to acknowledge each other. My baby sister often talked with him and kept the rest of us informed. Now he's dead. He was only 56 years old but he looked every bit of 80.

I took off work for the funeral and asked Kathy to stay with Rachel the days I was away. I didn't want Mom around his people alone. They were still upset with her for leaving him. To them, the man could do no wrong. I wanted to be there in case someone had something to say to her. We arrived in Jackson two days before the funeral. We had a lot to do the day of the funeral. All of the children were sitting front and center. There was kindness on both sides and there was animosity as well. He had one cousin that was rolling her eyes and staring unnecessarily. I stared her down to let her know that I was not intimidated. I felt sorry for WJ, but he made his bed and now he had to lie in it. Over all everything went well. I had to hurry back. The rest of the family was staying an extra day. Rachel could go into labor at anytime. I wanted to be there when it happened. J.J. was even more excited about this pregnancy than I was. We decided if it was a boy his name would be Randy and if it were a girl her name would be Brandy. I knew Kathy was walking on pins and needles. She really didn't care much for Rachel but she went out of her way to be kind just for me and I really appreciated it. The flight was scheduled to take off in two hours. My car was at the airport parking lot. I had paid for everyone's round trip tickets. The drive home for J.J. and me was pretty quick. Kathy and Rachel were very happy to see me. I wanted a bath and a good nights sleep. I couldn't get WJ out of my mind. I never wanted to lose my family the way he lost his. I made small talk with Kathy and then put J.J. to bed. After Kathy left, Rachel was all over me.

"I know you feel bad about your father. Let me make it better." Rachel believed sex made everything better. Even looking as though she would go into labor at anytime she always wanted to make love. The woman never had a headache or any other sign of sickness. Sometimes I wish she would just so I could get a little rest. Don't get me wrong I can hold my own in bed but it's just that I have been putting in long hours at work lately. In addition to that I'm also afraid of hurting her.

"Come on James. You know what I need." That was all she needed to say. Rachel could light my fire anytime and she knew it. It didn't take much to satisfy her and sometimes I was the one who was left wanting more. I would tell myself that I would make up for it after the baby came.

THE STORK MAKES A DELIVERY

The moment of truth came two nights later. We were playing around when I felt the bed and found that it was wet. We were both laughing. She was having a little pain but nothing to get alarmed about. I called Dr. Allen right away. She said she would meet us at the hospital in one hour. After arriving at the hospital she was checked in immediately and taken to the delivery room to give birth. She was very calm. I was even more relaxed for after all this was her first time and my second. I wanted to take pictures but we decided not to. Rachel was in labor all of 30 minutes. Dr. Allen gave the baby to me while announcing it was a boy. He weighed 6 ½ lbs. and was 21 inches long. I must say he was a good-looking kid. He was my second son so why wouldn't he look good? The first thing out of my mouth was, "Randy. Dr. Allen is he healthy?"

"He is as healthy as they come."

The nurse was smiling. "He has everything; 10 toes, 10 fingers and a very nice set of lungs." He was crying so loud, he could be heard clear down the hall.

They put him in my arms first and I took him over to Rachel. I was sure my mind was playing tricks on me but it seemed as if she really didn't want to hold him.

"James, I just want to get some sleep." I think the nurse picked up on it too.

"She is just tired Mr. Bradshaw. She will fill different tomorrow." I said okay and I held Randy for a moment. They say the baby bonds with the first person they come in contact with and that was me in this instance. By the hospital having what is called a family labor room, every body could see him. Mom, Kathy, Liz and Bobby were there to see our bundle of joy. Dr. Walls came just before the baby arrived. They could see the baby. Everyone was very happy. Mama initiated conversation.

"God takes one, but he always replaces them with another life." Everyone decided to go home but I was staying the night. The next morning the nurse brought the baby in to be fed. I took the bottle and did the feeding. Rachel made it plain that she wasn't going to breast-feed and this time I was sure judging by her actions. When I confronted her she burst into tears and said she just wasn't sure about this and she didn't want this baby to come between us.

"Look I asked for this! Now if you are going to remind me everyday that the child is not my blood then maybe I did make a mistake but I don't think so. Look he loves me. We are a two-some. I guarantee if I feed him long enough he will begin to look just like me." We both started laughing. This time she took the baby and there was affection between mother and child. I could feel an attachment happening for them. From then on she was better with Randy but she had a lot to learn about being a mother. Mom and Kathy were there to lend a helping hand. Liz even came around more often. She was crazy about Randy. The kid was so popular that he already had a bank account.

It wasn't long before it was time for Rachel's six-week check up. Her doctor's appointment was that Thursday and we had a date that Saturday night. I got off early, took a shower, and put on black pants with a gray pull over one body sweater. Rachel had on (you guessed it) pink and gray. A tight gray skirt and a pink sweater with every curve showing for all too see. She finally had her body back. We went to the Dome for dinner first which was a very nice place. I wanted this evening to be special. We checked into the Radisson Hotel. No phone, no kids, no family, and no patients, just her and me. I had room service to chill the champagne just before we arrived. It still wasn't my favorite but I could tolerate it better cold. Rachel went to slip into something more comfortable. It was a black negligee that left nothing for the imagination. Man. God bless America. This woman was so fine I could kiss her Daddy. I made two steps and was across the room with her in my arms. It was as if I was seeing my wife for the first time. This time I was the aggressor. I stood in the middle of the floor. I felt her lips tentatively touch mine; her tongue gently demanded admission and I felt something rise. I had to get a grip. I felt her shuddering response and then the kiss turned to passion. I could feel her body tremble against mine. I could feel the heat with each kiss. She arched toward me welcoming each touch. I kissed her eyes, her ears, and then her throat. When I groaned a low animalistic sound she trembled again. I wanted her and I know she wanted me. This beautiful woman is my wife and it seemed as if we are together for the very first time. I didn't want to rush this and I wanted it to last. I pulled back just to study her face. She buried her face in my chest. I pulled the string on the negligee. It started to fall away from her body and I could feel her bare rib cage. The nightie fell lower until it was around her ankles. In one movement she lifted her foot and nudged it off her feet and away from us. I pushed her back and down onto the plush carpet. She went willingly. We were stretched out on the nappy fabric. I was all over her. My hand touched her cheek; my fingers traced the line of her chin and then touched her parted lips. She sucked gently on my fingers.

"God you're beautiful," I murmured in a raspy whisper. Then my hands found her breasts and the feeling of her body against mine was a heady sensation. It wasn't long before my mouth replaced my fingers on her breasts, teasing her nipple with my tongue. She moaned softly. My hand skimmed over her stomach. When I touched her center, she gasped arching suddenly when I pressed the palm of my hand against her. She cried out. With agonizing slowness I started to make circular movements against her.

"James, I need to feel you inside of me." Her words were unsteady. It's been so long since we could be with each other like this. She pulled me even closer and then over her. This time she was leading and I just followed. She lifted her hips inviting me to her. I felt her breathing stop as she was guiding me inside her. Her hips lifted again to receive me and as I began to move inside her, she rocked her body to my rhythm. There was no gentle building of sensations at that moment but a white-hot agony that seemed to possess me. As our movements got faster and faster, she clung to me digging her nails into my back as she held on for dear life. Just as I knew I couldn't take it any longer I felt that the ecstasy was going to shatter me. I heard Rachel cry out and then I heard my own voice mingled with hers. For that moment, a single heartbeat, I knew we had become a part of each other in a way we had never experienced before. I just lay there holding her tight in my arms until I heard her breath give way to the sound of sleep. Feeling very weak myself, I carried her to the bed and I fell off to sleep holding her in my arms.

STRANGE THINGS!!!!

I woke early but didn't feel well. I then realized that I didn't have to get up so early. I turned back over. I was unusually tired. I felt like something had been taken out of me. Rachel was like super woman. I was really weak. I wanted to stay in bed but we got up and took a bath, and history repeated itself. She was in charge. We had a good time but I felt like I had a bug or something. Rachel even did the driving home thank God. We had gone to a motel; not out of town. I think I would have flown home in that case. Rachel went to get the kids and I went to bed. The next day at work I still didn't feel much better. John said I looked like shit and told me to take the rest of the day off. I did. He didn't have to tell me twice. I went home and back to bed. Rachel was teasing me.

"Am I too much for you?" I couldn't say anything. I just laughed.

"I'll be back on my feet soon." I went to my doctor. He gave me a complete check up and some vitamins. I was still feeling bad. This went on for about two weeks and then I was sick every morning. John made a comment about what he thought it might be.

"If you were a woman, I would say you were pregnant but we both know that's impossible with you being a man. You never stopped to think that Rachel might be. Just kidding."

"Man get real we have a baby that's only 8 weeks old. We don't need another one right away."

Even Mom and Kathy were worried about me. I worked everyday but I was very sick for about 30 minutes every morning just like clockwork. This went on for a month. Randy was 12 weeks old. Rachel went for another check up only to find out that she was six weeks pregnant. Neither one of us could believe it because there were no signs or symptoms on her part. I was the only one going through sickness. She was very happy. Now our family will be complete. She would always say that or something like that.

"James this one is a girl. I just know it." I didn't say anything. I just wanted to feel better. After about another two weeks, I was feeling much better. Rachel never got morning sickness. How fortunate she was. She just wanted to eat. During her pregnancy with Randy she was always sick in the beginning. Mom and Kathy were crazy about Randy but they were also overjoyed about the new baby.

They were shopping every week for baby things. Everything was bought new. I couldn't understand because we had gotten everything new for Randy. Why couldn't the next child use some of the same stuff? I wasn't cheap but trying to deal in logic.

After about three or four months I was good to go. The morning sickness had passed and I was myself again. I could really say I got tired of hearing about this baby. For nine months, it was all about the baby. The baby this, the baby that. The way Rachel was acting you would have thought this was her child instead of our child. She had a natural childbirth. She wouldn't take anything. She only used Lanacane to assist with the stitches she had to get. The moment the baby was born she said, "Give me my baby." There was no doubt in my mind that she really wanted this child.

I couldn't understand but I guess it's a woman thing. Life went on. It looked as if four days out of the week Randy was with Mom and Kathy. Rachel was always paying attention to Brandy. They went as far as dressing alike. Brandy looked just like me. She should have been a boy. I was just happy that she was healthy. One day after Randy learned to talk real good. He called Mom, "Mommy." He always wanted to be with her, Kathy or Liz. If I was around, he was right there. He would leave all of us just to follow J.J. J.J. was his hero. J.J. could do no wrong and he felt the same about Randy. J.J. didn't spend much time with Brandy. He said she was spoiled. Mom made the comment one day that Rachel didn't act like she cared too much about Randy. She had better be careful. He is getting to the age where he can tell the difference. It will come back to haunt her one day.

Rachel was so protective of Brandy that only Mom, Liz or Kathy was allowed to baby-sit her.

Things were going well. I was constantly working hard on the job to continue to support our financial stability. I just wanted to make sure we had the things we needed. Rachel was working again. We really didn't need the money but she worked to remain active in the work force.

Everything seemed to be working in our favor. The kids were in school. I had just purchased a larger house: a five bedroom, 3 bath with a swimming pool. We did whatever it took to make our home enjoyable for us to live in. About a year later we got new neighbors, a mixed couple. He was black and she was white, Charles and Linda. They seem to be very nice but she was just a bit on the *trampy* side in my opinion. She was always half naked except for going to work. She was a nurse. Whenever I was out working in the yard she made it her business to come out and talk. The woman was starving for company. Charles would visit but not as often as his wife would. Rachel didn't seem to care much for him but her and Linda hit it off. She did comment once on the way Linda dressed. She asked me did I think Linda was cute?

I said, "She's okay. I am not into white or yellow women but she seem to be nice." That was the end of that.

I would cook out on Saturdays. John, his lady, my family, and Helen would all attend. Annie would come only if Helen came. Helen and I would talk about old times and the good old days. I began to notice that Helen would never bring a date. She never said anything but sometimes I could see something in her eyes. Once she did say, "James, I am happy that you are happy."

I asked once if she was seeing anyone. She just smiled and said, "I am a woman."

"Yes," I said. "A very lovely one at that." Charles came over and she walked away.

"Man, I really would like to get next to her. Who is she?"

"A very good friend. I thought you had everything you wanted in Linda."

"Yes. Linda is okay but we are not married."

"So get married. You do have a commitment with each other. You brought a house together."

"Correction. Linda is buying the house. I just pay half of everything else. The house is in her name only. If I fuck up I can just pack my shit and leave." He never bit his tongue about anything. If it came up then it was coming out. I was thinking to myself that Linda didn't trust him very much and with good reason. Maybe she knew something that I didn't. From what I picked up from Rachel, Linda came from a well to do family that didn't care much for Charles. It was not because he was black but because he didn't have plans for the future. I think I saw Linda differently after that day. We always talked. I could see she really was in love with Charles but living with the fear that he would leave her for some one else. Charles had another woman and he left her for Linda. I didn't want to be the one to tell her that he would leave her someday because it was in his nature judging by how he went from one relationship to another.

IF IT ISN'T ONE THING, THEN IT'S ANOTHER

I didn't get to talk to Linda much after that. I had a little chaos in my world. Betty called Kathy asking her for my number. Out of respect for my wife she made sure she didn't give her my home number. She gave her my work number. She could call Liz, Kathy or Mom. It seemed as if she had a change of heart and she wanted to see J.J. for a weekend. She said she would be in Florida this week. I said okay thanking God I had told him all about her 6 years ago. Mom and Kathy said this would happen. I picked him up from school and told him. "Do I really have to? Can you come along to?"

"No because this is time for you and your mom to be alone with each other."

"No Daddy, it's not Mom, it's Betty. She wants me to call her Betty and her Mom Auntie Marie." I didn't make any comments on that. I knew Betty loved, J.J. but she was still Marie's little girl after 30 years. Betty came to Pick J.J. up. Except for pictures and TV I hadn't seen much of her for the past 11-½ years. She looked good. Rachel was very impressed with her. She was talking a mile a minute. It took four years before I would admit Betty was J.J.'s mother to her. Betty went by to see Mom and Kathy. Betty always made it a point to see Annie. She long ago accepted the fact that Annie was her aunt. Betty was Marie's daughter but she had her grandfather's heart.

We got through the weekend all right. I was restless. J.J. got home around 8:30 Sunday night. He was very tired but said he had a good time. Rachel wanted the 411 but I told him to go to bed.

The next day, Betty called me at work to say hello and thank you. "There is no need for you to thank me. He is your son."

"James do you think that maybe we could have lunch together sometime?"

"Betty I'm not sure if that will be such a good idea." She was quiet for a moment and said, "You are still a one woman's man. James, I was a fool to let you get away but I guess one can't have everything one wants when one wants it."

"Yes. You wanted your career."

"Yes, but you have a career and a family. I had never heard of nephrology until I read about you in the Health Digest. James, I'm really proud of you. I am so happy that J.J. has a father like you and we will always be friends. James, I want you to know that I will always love you. I never stopped. I was too young and stupid to know what I had in you."

I was sitting there listening and I realized that this was my closure with Betty. We would always be friends. After our talk I was able to get my thoughts back to my family. I realized I needed this conversation.

When I got home, Charles and Linda were sitting on the patio with Rachel. She knew if it was one thing I hated is company at my house when I get home. I said hello, made small talk, and excused myself. I just wanted to take a shower and get a little reading done. I was working on a new subclavian. We were running into problems with the last two. I had something in mind and that's when I heard a knock at the door.

"Yes." It was Rachel.

"James, are you coming back outside?"

"No. I have a lot of work to do." She knew me well enough to let it go. She went back to her guests. I went back to work. I got a lot done. I stayed in my study until after midnight. When I went to bed, Rachel was asleep and I was grateful for that. I didn't want to discuss the early afternoon events.

I was up early. I was ready for the meeting. I was at work half an hour before everyone else. I thought John had come in right behind me. We both smiled. He had coffee.

"I knew you would be here," he said. I gave him the proposal so he could look it over.

"Yes!" We did a high five. "James, you have outdone yourself. I know the board will go for it."

Sure enough the board ate it up. We got another budget of $5,000,000. Now we could expand the unit to 10 chairs. I left the job very happy which only lasted until I got home. Upon arriving there, Charles was once again sitting in my living room. He always got home around 2:30 or 3:00 p.m. Even though I set my own hours, I didn't leave the office until 4:00 or 5:00 p.m., sometimes later. I didn't say anything but I was tired of coming home to find him at my house. Rachel was off work with a sprained ankle. It was him or Linda that seem to always drop by but him more so than she was lately.

James do you want a beer?" He hollered out as I passed by him.

"No, man. I have some papers to look over. You help yourself."

"Don't mind if I do." He and Rachel laughed a kind of laugh that meant he worked too hard.

By the time I showered and changed he was gone. Rachel confronted me and decided to let me have it.

"You are so antisocial. You never want to enjoy my friends." I got upset instantly.

"Your friends? You said you couldn't stand the man. Now every time I come home he is at my table or on my couch watching TV? Does he still have a job? Or is he working here?" By this time we were both screaming. The kids came running in to see what was wrong. All three children came straight to me.

"Daddy what's wrong?" Rachel gave me a look that said you are taking my children away from me. Lately we have been at each other's throats. I couldn't do anything to please her. Liz and Kathy had picked up on the bad vibes that existed between us. Even John knew home wasn't home any more. I couldn't pin point when it started but I know it's been going on for a month. She would constantly say she was tired of just going to work, church, movies, and staying home. "I need some excitement in my life," she would say. She didn't even spend much time with Brandy and everything got on her nerves. This went on for a few more weeks. I would take her out to the movies or to dinner. It wasn't enough for her. I offered to go away on a weekend trip with her and she said no indicating that it wouldn't be any fun. Nothing was ever enough. Things continued to get worse.

CAUGHT ON FILM

We had been married 6 years when I got sick one day at work, which was unusual. John said, "Go home and stay there until you are better."

I was almost home and my mind said do not pull into the driveway. I followed my right mind and parked in front of the neighbor's house. Just as I was about to call out her name, I heard the music. Rachel loved the blues especially when we were making love. Only this time we weren't making love. Then I heard voices, both male and female. It was Rachel and Charles. My wife and my neighbor. Rachel was all into it, which was something that hadn't occurred between us in quite a while. I pushed the bedroom door open just to get a good look. I had a thousand thoughts going through my head. Some made sense and some didn't. One thought said get your gun so you can blow them both away. The other thought was to get one of Juju's cameras and capture the moment on film. All I could see was flesh. I knew my wife was a freak but this was enough to make a man kill. They were going at each other like it was going to be the last time. She kept calling him Daddy. That was the same thing that she used to call me. I could hear him say, "Tell me I'm the best."

"You are the best," she said in her most seductive voice.

When I got my feet and mind to work together I stepped backward and out of the room quietly. They didn't even notice that I was there. I went to J.J.'s room and got his Polaroid camera. There was some outside force working within me. It was a force that I couldn't understand. I could hear Papa Joe saying that no woman is worth going to jail for. I got the camera. I didn't even think about the gun again and besides it was in the garage. They were so in to it that I had taken five pictures before they heard the click and became aware of the flash. Thank God for my son's hobby. He took pictures of everything. Sometimes I would get upset about the camera but now I was thanking God that it was there and already loaded with film. Charles was the first to look into my eyes. I got a picture of that too. She had her back toward me. She was on top.

"Oh my God, James. Man, I am…." That was as far as he got. Rachel was screaming as if I had hit her or something. Don't think for one second that I didn't want to. I will never forget her words.

"What are you doing here? I live here remember. This is my house." By this time I was screaming,

"Get your clothes on and get out!! Both of you!! Get out!!!" Rachel ran toward me. I jumped back like she was a ball of fire.

"James please we need to talk. I don't know why this happened." By this time Charles was gone. "James please, where will I go?"

"I don't know, nor do I give a damn. You have one hour to get out of my house." I was so hurt and mad that I didn't trust myself to be around her any longer. "Just get out Rachel."

"What about my kids?"

"Now you think about them? Remember they are my kids too. We will let the court decide." I got in my car, and I drove around for about an hour. Then I went to Randy and Brandy's school. It was 11:00 a.m. They would be very happy to get out early. What would I say to them after they found out that their mother was gone? Then I remembered Brandy telling me a few times that Uncle Charles was there when they came home from school, but I never paid much attention to her. She was only 5 years old. I went by the principal's office and signed the children out of school.

"Is anything wrong Mr. Bradshaw?"

"No. I just have the day off, and I would like to take them to a movie and lunch."

"That's good. I wish we had more fathers like you." I really wanted to make sure that Rachel didn't get them and try to leave town. With the pictures I had I knew I would get custody and I would make sure she didn't get a dime. I took the kids to a movie. They had been bugging me to see 101 Dalmatians for as long as I can remember. I was still running a temperature but I had to call my lawyer. After we got home around 2:30 p.m., the house was empty. J.J. was due home at 3:30 p.m.

Randy asked, "Where is Mom?"

I could only say, "Mom is gone. She went away for a while."

Randy shocked me by saying, "Dad did Mom go away with Charles?" Randy was 6 years old and just as smart as any 10-year-old.

"Why do you ask son?"

"I saw Mom and Uncle Charles kissing and they said they were going on a trip together without you and Linda."

"When did you see and hear this?"

"Last week when we had a half day and Mrs. Scott brought us home because Mom forgot to pick us up and Uncle Charles was here." I wanted to say stop calling him uncle but I didn't want to confuse the children by interrupting their routine. I went into my study and called Bob Conningham, my lawyer. I told him the entire story and said, "I want my kids. She can see them once or twice a month, but no more than that. I want a divorce as soon as possible; like yesterday."

"I'm drawing up the papers. I will get a court date right away. Don't worry James, you will get the kids but just hold on to the pictures."

Now was the hard part. I called Liz. She was still living alone. I asked her to come over. I had to talk to her. Luckily she was on vacation for two weeks. I needed her to watch the kids. I had some thinking to do. I called John also. I didn't get into all the details but he knew something was seriously wrong.

The next day Liz got the kids off to school. I was at the bank when it opened. I cancelled all the credit cards that were in both of our names. I closed out the joint checking account that I opened for us. Everything was mine. I just added her name when we got married. I wanted her off of everything immediately. When I was finished, it looked as if she never existed. From day one I had made sure she had her own checking and savings. I just added her on mine also. I made sure every week that she put away one or two hundred dollars. I didn't ask how much she had or how often she put money into the account. That's the way Kathy had explained it to me. Now I am very happy I did it that way. She couldn't say I took anything from her. I really hope she was a smart woman because she would need her money.

I wasn't in a hurry to talk to anyone. The kids didn't have many questions. They were more aware of what went down then I was. I knew I should have dealt with my feelings, but it was too hard to face reality right now. Besides, I was young, successful, and I tried really hard to take care of my wife. I come home and find her balling my neighbor. Hell this was a hard pill to swallow by any means. I don't know how I got through the rest of the week, but I made it.

That Saturday the phone rang. I wasn't expecting anyone until after 2:00 p.m. I was having a cook out. I would explain my problems all at once, and I didn't want to have to explain it again after that. It was only a little past 10:00 a.m. I answered the phone. It was Dr. Walls.

"James, how are you?"

"Oh, I'm fine." I paused for a second. I already had my guards up because I didn't know what he was getting ready to say.

"James, may I stop by? I could be there in ten or fifteen minutes. I really need to talk to you. It won't take long. Rachel called me but there are two sides to every story. We might as well get this out into the open."

"Okay. Come on."

"Thanks."

I liked Dr. Walls but he always seemed to be so sad. Rachel wasn't very nice to her father but he was okay with me. Dr. Walls arrived at about 10:30 a.m.

"How are you doing?"

"I'm okay."

"James if there's anything I can do for you or the kids please don't hesitate to call me. James, I've wanted to talk to you for a long time. I mean really talk to you but Rachel made me promise to just let sleeping dogs lie. She didn't want me to tell you what happened to her mother. I first want to emphasize that I had nothing to do with Barbara's death. She killed herself after I found out about her and my best friend. She just couldn't live with the guilt. I tried to talk to Rachel about it but she was passed understanding. It was easy for her just to blame me for everything. To keep at least half a relationship with my daughter, I let her have her own beliefs. Ruth, Rachel's sister, was older and she knew and understood what was going on. She even caught them in the act one time. Barbara didn't see her. Ruth and I are very close, but Rachel is just in love with my money." There was a lot of pain in his eyes. I could tell that Rachel reminded him of Barbara. "James, I've heard bits and pieces of what happened. Will you tell me what really happened? I know I will get the truth from you."

"Sure." I gave him a cup of coffee and I told him the entire ugly story trying not to leave anything out or add anything unnecessary. I didn't wait for the others. I will tell them later.

"Son, I know this will be hard for a while but the pain will go away. I know the timing is not the best but do you think I could see more of my grandchildren?"

I knew Rachel only let him see them once in a while. She could be a real bitch.

"Sure. I am having a cook out today after 2:00 p.m. why don't you just stay here or come back later when all the guests have arrived. I have some jeans and a sweatshirt that you could put on. "

"You don't mind if I stay?"

"No. The kids will be happy to see you. They will be up in a little while. I let them stay up late last night. I am not going out."

"I will get the fire started for you. I'm also a pretty good cook if you need my assistance. I can go to the store for you if there's anything else you need for the cook out."

"Mr. Walls, calm down. I have everything I need. Just make yourself at home. I will get the kids up."
J.J. was the first one in the room.

"Granddad how are you? What brings you over? Randy and Brandy will be glad to see you."

I never could understand why J.J. got along with Dr. Walls but he could take Rachel or leave her.

J.J. asked, "Are you staying for the cook out today?"

"Yes your father invited me to stay."

"Great. We're going to have a lot of fun. Maybe we can play a game of chess."

Roger taught J.J. how to play and he was very good at it. By this time Randy and Brandy had gotten up, it sounded as if we were already having our own party. All you could hear was grandpa this and grandpa that. No one mentioned Rachel. I got everything ready for the barbecue. I realized that I did have to go to the store for a few items. Roger stayed with the kids while I went to the store for a few items.

Neither kid wanted to follow me, even J.J. Grandpa saved the day. It wasn't long before Kathy, Annie, and Helen arrived. Mom called to say she and the rest of the family were on their way. I was flipping burgers when Bobby walked in. "I'm ready to eat."

"You're always ready to eat."

"James, where's the beer?"

"On ice of course. I'll get it. I want to talk to everyone first while I have a clear head because I'm only going to say this once. I don't intend to repeat myself and I'm going to have a few beers! Just a few!"

"Okay man, I get your drift."

Mom and the rest of the family were there by then. Kathy and Roger were having a good conversation and playing with the kids. It was kind of funny to hold a meeting about you and you're soon to be ex-wife's problems especially with her father present. At the same time, I wanted to get the bad news out of the way.

"Okay. Let me have everyone's attention. As you all know Rachel and I are getting a divorce." All eyes went to Roger. I spoke again. "Roger is aware of the situation between us and I am sure if put in the same position he would have done the same. Roger is a part of this family. These are his grandchildren and I would never do anything to try to take that away from him. He is welcome here anytime. Maybe now he can see more of the kids." The look on his face said it all. I could see thank you in his eyes. "Rachel and I are going to court next week. The judge will decide who will get custody of the children. That's all I can say for now. Now I want everyone to have a good time. I didn't cook all this food for it to go to waste."

Roger pulled me aside and said, "James please fight for the kids. I love my daughter, but I don't feel right about her having the children. She is unable to be a good mother right now. I will stand by you. I am not going to see Rachel homeless but I'm going to stand on the truth and what's right. Get the kids."

Somehow hearing those words from Roger brought us closer together. I had his support. I just couldn't see tearing a family apart just because the husband and wife couldn't make it. The way I see it, the grandparent have rights also.

We had a very good time. By the time everyone went home it was 8:30 p.m. Roger gave Annie and Kathy a ride home. Helen stayed behind to help me clean up and get the kids to bed.

"James, I really wish you the best in court next week."

I wanted to take her in my arms but refrained from it realizing that this was neither the time nor the place. I walked her to her car and said good night. I wanted to say more but I could wait. Later on as I thought about my life I realized the job was calm. John tried to get me to take a vacation but I wouldn't hear of it.

I felt it was in my best interest to keep busy. I had less time for thinking.

LET THE TRUTH BE TOLD

Just before going into the courtroom, Kathy and Rachel faced off. I didn't see it coming. Rachel walked up to Kathy and accused her of telling me things about her.

"Let me tell you something you little whore. I didn't tell him anything. If I had, maybe he would have caught you months ago. Everyone knew except him. You didn't have enough sense to keep it out of your kids' face. They may be young but they are not stupid. Face it Rachel you got just what you deserved."

All I could do was keep Liz off of Rachel. Kathy told Liz, "Don't worry she is stupid but she's no fool. If she lays one finger on me this bitch will never ever get out of jail." I was seeing another side of Kathy that I had never seen before. I think Jack was wrong. Kathy could definitely hold her own. The bailiff came out and said to keep it down. We were the next case on the docket.

"James," Kathy said in a much calmer voice, "she is referring to the fact that there were several times I went by to see the kids only to find them outside and the house locked. One time she came to the door without clothes on and Charles came out behind her. I guess they weren't thinking, just didn't care, or maybe drunk. I never went back again. That was about 3 months ago." I was thinking that explains why Kathy stop coming over except for when I had cookouts. "Ida and me talked about it but we didn't want to see you hurt. We knew she would get caught sooner or later and sure enough she did. So you see I didn't have to say anything. You did it to yourself."

By this time the bailiff was leading us in. We were seated and the judge was looking over the case.

"Will the counsel state your case, please."

"Your Honor, Mr. Bradshaw is filing for divorce and is requesting that custody of his children be granted to him on the grounds of adultery on Mrs. Bradshaw's part."

"Your Honor, Mrs. Bradshaw admits to making a small mistake, but she is a good mother and wants custody of the children to be granted to her."

"Your Honor, Mr. Bradshaw is in a better position to take care of the kids."

"Your Honor, Mrs. Bradshaw is not working at the time but she is counter suing for alimony which will leave her comfortable and financially secure enough to raise her children in the manner which she is used to."

The judge took all of five minutes to make up his mind.

"I am awarding full custody……………"

That was as far as he got and Rachel started screaming like a crazy woman.

"You can't take Randy!!! You are not his father!! I want my son!!"

"Order. Order. Order in the court!!" The judge was shouting. It was very quiet all of a sudden.

At that moment I could have killed her. The judge sat back and cleared his throat.

"Please remove the children from the courtroom."

Liz took the kids out. Once the kids were removed from the courtroom, the judge continued with his ruling.

"Mrs. Bradshaw, one more outburst like that, and I will have you removed from the court room! I am looking over the files and Mr. Bradshaw is listed as the father on each birth certificate. In my opinion that makes him the father of the children. If a man takes on the responsibility of a child as his own, I think it would be in poor taste for you to get up in court and seek to rip that father and child apart."

 "Mrs. Bradshaw, Mr. Bradshaw will have complete custody of the children and your visitation rights can be worked out between the two of you. It is in the best interest of the children that they remain with Mr. Bradshaw who can properly provide for them and raise them in a stable home. There will be no alimony granted to Mrs. Bradshaw."

"But I want my kids!!!"

"After a thorough review of this file including the photos and the charges brought against you, I don't think you had your children in mind. Court is dismissed. Mr. Bradshaw please make sure you make the court aware of the visitation arrangement. If you have any problems call your lawyer or the local police and they will know exactly what to do."

They pulled Rachel away screaming. "James, you made me do it. If you had been a better husband and spent more time with me, I wouldn't have done it."

I did as the judge said and took my kids home. Later that night, Randy came into my room. The little guy had tears in his eyes. It seemed as if he and J.J. had a talk first.

"Daddy what did mama mean about you not being my father? Daddy why did she say that?" I wanted to say that she was lying but I said I would tell the truth if he ever asked. I just had no idea I would be explaining this to a 6-year-old. I took him in my arms and asked him, "Do you know what adoption means?"

"Yes. My friend Omar is adopted."

"Is he happy?"

"Yes. His adopted parents are very good to him."

"Does he love them?"

"Yes, Daddy. They are his family."

"Well, Randy that's the way you and me are. I adopted you before you were born. Your mother was pregnant when I met her."

"You didn't mind?"

"Well, I didn't know it until a month later and by that time I was in love with her, so I was willing to accept the entire package."

I tickled him like I always do and he was laughing.

"Do you think you will ever stop loving me?"

"No. Of course not."

"You adopted me so you are my real dad. That's what Omar would say."

"I guess Omar is a pretty smart kid."

"He is. Dad you know what?"

"What?"

"I am glad you adopted me and I am glad Grandma Ida and Grandma Kathy loves me too." By this time I was really trying to fight back the tears that were coming so I didn't trust myself to speak. I picked him up and took him to his bed. J.J. was already asleep. I tucked Randy in and checked on Brandy. I turned in for the night. I made up my mind to sell the house and move back to the old house with Liz so the kids would be right across the street from school. J.J. would be there for half the year. He would be in the seventh grade next year.

I got up the next day and called John. I said I was taking the rest of the week off. I called Liz to make sure she didn't mind having company at her house.

"No, you know I will love having my kids back. When are you moving?"

"Today and tomorrow. I think I will start right now." The kids were beside themselves with joy. "I never really liked this house. I bought it to make Rachel happy. I prefer the house Jack left me in his will. I will have it remodeled and add two rooms."

"James what are we going to do with all that furniture you have?"

"I think we should sell it. Get dressed and come over here."

MOVING UP AND OUT

I fixed the kids breakfast and made a few signs. After Liz arrived I went and made copies to hang a few at the supermarket as well as a few areas that will draw some attention. I arrived back at the house and started pulling things out into the yard in preparation for the sale. Liz assisted me in putting a price on things. I had no idea what to charge. The only thing I knew was that I paid good money for everything. By the end of the day, we had sold just about everything. We only made about $2800 but that was better than nothing. There was a lifetime of memories associated with that stuff but I was willing to let go of all of them. I knew there was no turning back. I never told anyone but I never slept in the bed after Rachel left that day. I washed everything over and over again but I could never use the sheets or any of the linen after what I saw. As a matter of fact I sold that also. I didn't sell any of Rachel's clothes. I asked her to come and get them but she didn't so

Liz packed them up and put them to one side in one of the rooms.

Liz left the kids room just as I left them. I took the den for the time being. I knew it would only be for a few weeks.

That Friday I found a construction company and called them to come out and give me an estimate on the work that I wanted to have done. I wanted to turn away from the estimate but this was for my kids so I agreed to it. The weekend passed swiftly.

If Liz called me once she called me six times during the day. The construction crew was working fast. This was the first day of construction and by Friday I knew they would be finished. I was very busy at work for things had begun to pick up. We were scheduled to open a new clinic in another local hospital so this meant long hours. With Liz at the house, I didn't have to worry about my kids.

Rachel didn't call once during this time. The construction crew was running a little behind so it would be an extra four days with the rain and the weekend. I got through the construction and the opening of the new clinic. I worked hard but I found time for my kids especially Randy. Some nights he would get up after hearing me come in or he would be asleep in my bed. Liz said she put him to bed but he would get up and come into my room. I promised myself when this was over I was taking the kids on a vacation.

A week later I went by the old house to check the mail and just to take a look around. As I walked around the back, there was Linda. She was sitting there crying her eyes out. I walked over to her and started to comfort her.

"Hello. Linda I am very sorry about what happened between you and Charles, but you have got to get yourself together, chalk it up as experience and get on with your life. There are other men out there. You can't just draw up and die. The way you are headed you will set yourself up for another let down. Have you a good cry, take a few days off work, and get yourself together. You can start by getting rid of everything that reminds you of him like I did. I am going on with my life." I knew Linda would make it because she was a fighter. I said my goodbyes and left. I knew she needed some time alone.

It didn't take long for word to get around that Rachel and Charles were living together. They got a place together on the West Side. They weren't living in the best area in the world but it was livable. I drove by one day just to see where my children were going when they visited. I did speak to her. I could tell Charles was using drugs but I wasn't sure about Rachel. I would hope she is staying clean for the sake of the children. One thing I was very sure of though was that she looked pretty bad. She resembled a homeless person who hadn't had anything to eat in days. Things were going well with me. I even gave her a few dollars from time to time.

About one year later Roger and Kathy had become very good friends. As a matter of fact, they were dating. Helen was a nurse at Fairmont. Her, Annie, and Kathy still lived together. Mom and Kathy were still into everything and knew everybody's business. They knew stuff before it got to anyone else. I guess that's why it wasn't a surprise when both of them showed up at my door to say that Rachel was pregnant again.

"Well I am happy for her. Roger is not!" Kathy said.

"She can't take care of herself. How will she take care of another child?"

"Kathy the woman does work. She has an education in business." I was about to say more when Kathy voiced her own comment.

"Roger is devastated. He wanted so much better for her and have you seen Charles lately? He looks as if he is drying up day by day." I knew Roger kept Kathy and Mom up talking about Rachel's life. She was always calling asking him for money or to use his car. He went as far as purchasing one for her. It was a good car but now it looked like a piece of junk. Kathy was still talking when I decided to put my two cents in.

"Ladies I am very happy to get Rachel update 101 but I have better things to do with both my time and my life"

"James, you need to get out and start dating. You need to meet people your own age and get out more. James we all know that you have just centered your life on your kids. When you are not at work, you are at one of the kid's school."

"Mom I have time. I will meet someone some day." Kathy and Mom looked at each other, laughed and left without saying another word.

I had to spend time with my kids. I wanted them to know that I love them. Time passes by so fast that you look up and don't know where it went. I want to cherish these moments with my children because time will not reverse itself to let me see and value what I have missed. Rachel had only tried to see them four times in the past year and a half. My kids were growing fast and approaching adulthood. Soon I would be letting them go to be on their own. J.J. was in the eleventh grade at 14 and a half. It is his desire to become a doctor. He was working hard to get into medical school. Randy had a fascination with space and the stars. There was no doubt in my mind that he wanted to be an astronaut and you can bet that I will be pushing him every step of the way. We don't use the words "if" and "can't." In their place are "can" and "will." We will also use "going to" and "always try." Randy acts so much like me that one comments on it. He looks like me too. Maybe it's true what they say. If you feed them long enough, association brings on assimilation.

IS LOVE BETTER THE SECOND TIME AROUND?

After another month of feeling sorry for myself, I decided to try to get back into dating. It's not easy on a 32-year-old man. I didn't know where to start. My sister had an idea.

"Mann why don't you call Helen. You know she still has the hots for you."

"No!"

"Yes she does. Why don't you call her? I know you still find her attractive. I don't know what is taking you so long. Your brain is probably clogged up from lack of nookie syndrome. It's not normal to keep it inside." Liz had a way with words.

"I take it that you are getting your needs met?"

"I sure am. There are a few things I will do without, but sex is not one of them. If you don't use it, you lose it and besides what are you saving it for? You can't take it with you."

I did call Helen and surprisingly she agreed to go out with me. We agreed to meet at 7:00 p.m. tomorrow. I didn't say anything to Liz before going to bed nor did I say anything to John or anyone else for that matter. Over all it was a good day. I left work at 4:00 p.m. sharp, got home, took a bath, and got dressed. I must say I still had it going on. I didn't look bad considering I still had my hair and a nice white set of teeth.

I decided to drive the Mercedes. Liz and John talked me into getting it six months ago. They said it made me look prosperous, whatever that means. I pulled up in front of her house, got out and went to the door. Kathy and Annie weren't home. Helen answered after I rang the bell the first time. She was wearing a mint green pantsuit that hugged her like a plastic bag.

"Well hello, James. How is life treating you?"

She was so formal. I'd just run into her about two weeks ago at work and had small talk with her when I saw her with Kathy and Annie. It never crossed my mind to ask her out then. I just took it for granted that she had other things going for her. I knew she could do better than a man with three kids.

We went to dinner and then to a movie. Afterward we parked the car and went walking along the beach. I had forgotten how good it was to really talk to Helen. We really did have a lot in common. For example, she loved the medical field and so did I? At about 11:30, I took her home because we both had to work the following day. I wanted to take her into my arms but I didn't want to seem desperate. At the same time I didn't want to appear uninterested either. At her front door, I gave her a long kiss before I walked her in. I said hello and then good night to Kathy. It was no surprise to me that she was waiting up.

"Mom where is your side kick?" I said smiling. She was laughing and blushing at the same time.

"He just left. Honey I want you to have a cookout two weekends from Saturday. It's important that you get the family together because I have an announcement to make. You might as well invite Rachel also. She is still a part of this family." Rachel was coming by more now.

"Is there something I should know?"

"I will tell you then." I didn't tell her that Roger showed me the ring that he bought for her. He was going to ask her to marry him. I guess she said yes. She still looked good for her age. Mom was fifty-one, but Kathy was fifty-six. Jack was eight years older than she was. I just looked at Helen. She smiled and walked away.

"Okay. You got it. I will call everybody and plan to do a little cooking."

I called out to Helen and asked if we could have lunch tomorrow.

"Yes. I will meet you in the cafeteria at about 1:30 p.m."

"I will be there."

I was about to leave when Kathy came up to me and said in a low voice,

"I hope and pray that you and Helen get back together. You know she never stopped loving you and there has never been anyone else. Keep in mind that you didn't hear that from me."

"Okay. I will talk to you later on this week." I was out of there. On the ride home I couldn't forget what Kathy said. "There was never anyone else in Helen's life." I never saw her with anyone. She never brought a date to any of the cookouts. I didn't see her much in the hospital, but when I did she was alone or with a co-worker. She worked in geriatrics and I worked in nephrology. I promised myself that I would make it a point to bring that up tomorrow. I wanted to know for myself.

J.J. and Randy were up waiting for me when I got home.

"What are you two doing up this time of night? You have school tomorrow." J.J. spoke first.

"Okay. Dad are you finally getting together with Aunt Helen? All right! Way to go! Give me a high five!" He didn't wait for an answer.

"We went out. It was just a date. Who told you I went out with Helen?"

"Aunt Liz of course."

"Of course. Why doesn't that surprise me?"

J.J. was off to bed and Randy was all smiles.

"Daddy will you and Aunt Helen get married?" It was obvious that all of my kids were crazy about Helen.

"Would you like that?"

"Yes. I would love for Aunt Helen to be my mom, too."

"Well, we'll work on that. Now it's time to go to bed. You have school tomorrow." I tucked him in. J.J. was already asleep. I looked in on Brandy. She seemed to be okay. I turned in and went right to sleep.

I was up before the alarm clock went off. Liz was just getting off work. She would get the kids up and off to school.

"Well how did last night go?"

"It was just fine. We are having lunch today."

"Very good. Maybe this time you will get the right one."

"Let's not get into that. I'm going to let God work it out this time. I've tried the rest and now I am going to try the best."

Upon arriving at work the receptionist noticed something different about me.

"Are you alright?"

"Yes. Never better. Why do you ask?"

"Oh. No reason."

Next thing I know, John came in looking over his glasses.

"James, who is the new woman?"

I stopped and started laughing.

"What are you talking about?"

"James we have been working together over 10 years and I think I know you. I've seen you through marriage, divorce and two new kids. I know you. Now who is the lady?"

"Okay. Okay. I took Helen out last night and we had a very good time."

"Now was that a good time as in real good or as in real good and explosive?"

"Maybe real good and explosive. I didn't put the moves on her. You know me. If I am planning on some action, I want a weekend of it. If it's someone special and you know Helen is special, I just don't want to move in on her in case she has someone else."

"James this might come as a surprise to you, but there is no one else in Helen's life."

"How do you know?"

"We talk sometimes."

"You mean there has never been anyone else?"

"No. Not even someone to please her when needed."

"John that's been over 11 years."

"I am aware of how long it's been. James in case you don't know it, Helen never and I mean never stopped loving you. We all can see it. She's not the type to put the moves on a married man. She would always say that some day if it were meant to be then it would be. You were always wrapped up in work, Rachel, and the kids, which are understandable, but how you didn't notice I don't know. What made you ask her out?"

"Liz told me she was still carrying a torch for me."

"You see. Liz had to tell you. You were so blind that you didn't notice. You would never have picked up on it."

"Oh, I noticed all right. I noticed that every time I saw her I just felt that she deserved better than me."

"James, you deserve a good woman and Helen is a very good woman. Helen is the type of woman that will stand behind her man. You better wake up and smell the coffee before she gets away."

By the time 1:00 p.m. came I was nervous. I wasn't when we were together last night. I walked to the cafeteria very slow thinking about all the times I wanted to ask Helen out after things went bad with Rachel but I was afraid she would say no. I was sitting at a table in deep thought when Helen walked up.

"Ready to get something to eat before they close the lines?"

"Yes. That would be great."

We went to the lines where there was not much of a choice. I grabbed a sandwich while she had a salad. We went back to the same table because it was secluded which allowed us to talk without worrying about an outside listening ear. I initiated the conversation.

"Helen, I want to ask you something. I would appreciate if you would please tell me the truth."

"Okay. James just ask me. That shouldn't be a problem. You look so serious. What's wrong?"

"Helen, I don't know how to ask this so I'm going to just say it. Have you been dating since you and I had something and I mean really dating?"

"Why do you ask?"

"Helen, I need to know."

"James to be truthful, I went out a few times but nothing serious. I didn't want to get into anything that I didn't want. To answer your question, no I didn't get involved with anyone. I just put my feelings about our relationship in the back of my mind and focused on our friendship. James, I told you a long time ago that I just wanted to see you happy."

For the first time I understood true love. I understood the definition of loving and caring about another person. A lot of what Papa Joe said to me was becoming very clear to me at this very moment. Helen loved me unconditionally. Love is something that very few people ever experience.

"Helen, I am sitting here at a loss for words. I had no idea. I am sorry."

"James, you have nothing to be sorry for. You never asked me to put my life on hold for you. This is something that I chose to do on my own. First there was school and then my job. Annie got better and Kathy got her life back on track. I woke up one day and it was eleven years later. James, I have learned a lot. You see I know I don't need a man to make me happy. Don't get me wrong I would like to have one but I'm not going to die if I don't get one. Besides I keep plenty of batteries." We both laughed.

"Look I know we can't make up for loss time nor can we turn back the clock but if you let me, I really would like to progress from here."

We were just sitting there looking into each other's eyes when like magic our lips met. A few of the other tables were occupied and people were staring at us. I didn't care because the feeling I was experiencing I hadn't felt in years and I liked it. By the time lunch was over we had made plans to take some time off together and I had a few more surprises in mind. I would run them by J.J. tonight. He had become my advisor on women especially lately. At 15, he was in his last year of high school. I walked Helen back to her floor. I felt like a schoolboy for the first time in years. John was sitting on the edge of his seat of course. I had to fill him in on what was going on.

"I'm going to take some time off this weekend."

"Well good for you. What about Kathy's cook out?"

"That's next weekend. Thank God."

After work I went home and I found J.J. in my study. That's where he spends most of his time.

"Hi Dad. What's up?

"J.J., you know that I started dating Helen again and I wanted to know how you guys feel about that?"

"We just want to know what took you so long? I speak for all three of us."

"I want to see more of Helen. I mean a lot more of her. Maybe I would be more clear by saying I want to spend a life time together with her."

"Dad do you want to marry her?

"Yes? Great let's go pick out a ring."

"Just like that!"

"Let's go and pick out a ring. Yes just like that."

"She might say no."

"Dad can't you tell when a woman is crazy about you? Look how she treats us and how good she is to Mama and granny."

He called Kathy Granny but he called my mother, Mrs. Ida, mama. He never called Rachel anything but Rachel but Roger, her father, has always been grandpa.

"Dad, even I know, Aunt Helen is nuts about you."

"Boy what do you know at fifteen?"

"I know she really loves you. Now you want to go look at a few diamonds?"

We finally got up and went to the mall. I found a beautiful two and half carat that set me back three thousand dollars for the set.

"I think I am putting the cart before the horse. I have only been going out with her again for a week, really just talking. Maybe I should slow down a bit so she won't feel smothered."

"Dad how do you feel about Aunt Helen?"

"J.J., I wanted to marry her eleven years ago and she turned me down."

"That was then and this is now. How do you feel about her now?"

"You know I think you should be a lawyer instead of a doctor. I feel as if I'm being interrogated."

"Dad it's not too late to make plans for the weekend. Why don't you call Helen and see if you can get together for this weekend."

"J.J., you are smart beyond your years."

"I'm your son."

There wasn't much said on the drive back home. My own son had me at a lost for words. The world should watch out for my son. The minute I got in the house I called Helen. I wasn't sure if she had the weekend off or if she could get away. She picked up on the second ring. I just loved the sound of her voice.

A TRIP DOWN MEMORY LANE

"Helen, I know this is short notice but do you think you could get away for the weekend. I thought maybe if it's okay with you, we could get away and really iron out our feelings."

"Well, James this is my weekend off. I was planning on going to Tampa Bay to do a little shopping."

"I will come along. Maybe I can find something I like if it's Okay with you."

"I would love that."

"Okay. We will take my car. I will pick you up around 6:00 p.m. Friday."

"Goodnight James."

J.J. was standing in my doorway.

"So you have a date?"

"Yes we are going away for the weekend."

"Well, I will baby sit if Aunt Liz has something to do." By that time Liz walked in.

"Baby sit? Of course I will baby sit. Is Mr. Bradshaw going away for the weekend?"

"Yes, Miss Bradshaw he is."

"Well it's about time. I know you need it."

"I am going to bed you two. I am very tired."

I turned in and had no problem falling asleep. The next two days went very fast. By Friday, I was ready to get away. Mom and Kathy had done their homework. They both called me before I could get away just to wish us luck.

The trip only took two hours. We decided to stay at the Holiday *Dome*. This time of year it was easy to get a room. After we got inside I initiated conversation.

"Helen, I got us a suite. It has two bedrooms. I thought that would make things a little less intense for you."

"James, lets get serious. We are both adults so let's just see what happens. James just relaxes. We can play it by ear."

"Helen, I'm sorry but I am so nervous. I..........."

Before I could finish my sentence she was kissing me like I needed to be kissed.

"Relax baby. I will do the................"

She moved me over to the bed. With each step there was a kiss and a sustained word.

"Honey just forget the past. This is all new."

"Helen it has been a long time."

"I know James."

I looked deep into her eyes. I could see tears. I kissed her eyes and one fell.

"What's wrong baby?"

"It's been such a long time," she said. "There's been no one since..."

She left off the rest of the sentence but I know what she was trying to say. I hushed her with another kiss.

"Don't be afraid. I've probably forgotten what to do." She laughed gently.

"I understand it's just like riding a bicycle."

"The last time I rode a bicycle, I fell off and broke my arm."

"I won't hurt you Helen." I entwined my fingers in her hair. "I promise I won't hurt you."

We both relaxed and got comfortable. The next hours were spent exploring each other's bodies and reactions. The first time was sweet and gentle, the second heated and passionate, the third a combination of fire and tenderness….. I hadn't envisioned an entire night of passion and yet I'd been an equal participant. We talked a little. It was as though we were afraid that conversation would somehow break the spell.

"Tired?"

My head was propped up on one hand and I stroked Helen's brow with the fingertips of the other.

"A little. Mainly hungry. I haven't eaten since noon."

"Worked up an appetite, have you? Well I'd better get you a little sustenance woman because I want you to have plenty of energy for later." I was smiling at her.

I picked up the phone and made dinner reservations. She was looking at me puzzled.

"I didn't bring you here just to spend the weekend locked in this room. I am with the most beautiful woman in Florida and I want to show her off." She just smiled and said,

"I guess we had better get dressed."

We played as we dressed. I was guilty of stealing kisses and caressing her as she tried to apply fresh make up. It took over an hour for her to finish getting ready. We went downstairs to the dining room, which was located at the end of the pier jutting out onto the water. Huge windows provided a dramatic ocean view.

I ordered oysters on the half shell as an appetizer. "Insurance?" she said with a smile. I knew oysters were supposed to be an aphrodisiac, but judging by what had happened tonight I doubted either of us needed it. Just being together seemed to be enough.

We placed our order and then I ordered champagne.

"You're quiet." I took her hand. "Have I worn you out?" She gave me a weak nod. "I'm not used to............

"Having someone in your bed?" I smiled. "I'm not either you know. Although I think I could get used to it rather easily as long as you were that someone." I turned up the palms of her hands and gave each one a kiss. Dinner went well. We danced and danced.

When we returned to the suite, I immediately folded her in my arms. I was a little disturbed. The connection between us had been broken and I couldn't seem to get it back. If Helen sensed the change, she didn't comment on it. Yet when she headed toward her bedroom, I stopped her.

"Aren't you going to sleep with me? I want to hold you all through the night."

With her nestled in my arms in the darkened bedroom, I began to feel at peace. She was massaging my taut muscles, soothing them. She had apparently noticed the difference in my mood, but rather than talk about it, she had chosen to simply love me. She was giving, not taking … loving unselfishly. Our words were gentle, calming words of love.

"Your body is so beautiful. I've wanted to hold you like this for so long.… I love you James."

"I love you too," I answered, realizing for the first time that I truly did. When morning came we made love again and it really felt like making love.

Later we got up and took a shower and made love again. Our lovemaking was rough and intense, almost hurtful. Yet, when it was over and we lay side by side giving our spent bodies a chance to return to normal I said, "Helen I want you to marry me. I know you may need time to think about it. I have no problem giving it to you but please don't take too much. We shouldn't waste any more time. We've both wasted enough time as it is. We both waited too long."

"What about the children?"

"You know my children love you. Kathy, Annie, Mom, Liz and the rest of the family are just waiting to see if anything materializes from this weekend. Helen I know what I want and I want you. I'm not a twenty-three year old any more that you can use the future against. I am a man with three kids, a good job, and a very good income. You say you love me so what else is there?" I wasn't aware of how much rambling I was doing when she stopped me.

"James, James. Yes I will marry you!"

"You will! You really mean yes?"

"Yes, Yes, Yes, I will marry you.

"When can we set a date?"

"Don't you think we should get formally engaged first?" she was asking

"Yes. Hold on a minute." I went to my jacket and pulled out a little black and gold box. I got down on one knee and said, "Helen will you marry me?"

"James, you had this ring all the time!! You knew I would say yes?"

"No. I was hoping and praying you would say yes. J.J. helped me pick this out on Wednesday night."

"J.J. was in on this?"

"Yes. I guess you could say that."

"When should we set a date and tell the rest of the family?"

"Let's wait until the cookout coming up this next weekend for Kathy and Roger."

"Oh yes, the cook out. I'll start planning for that time when we return home. Well, young man we came here to get some shopping in, didn't we?"

"What do you say we start."

We both got dressed in jeans and a white polo shirt, which, was something I loved to do. I put all my money in my pocket and credit cards in my wallet in my back pocket. We walked and looked in a lot of stores. I just reached into my jean pocket when the sales person looked at me real strange just before I paid for my selections. At that moment I pulled out a wad of money. When they see that I have plenty of money they start biting at my butt and thinking about the commission they could make. I was insulted by their behavior so I put back half the stuff I had while they tried to talk me into keeping each item. I knew that what I was doing was not nice, but they should treat all customers the same. You never know who you might run into. We decided to walk and shop some more. Shopping was plentiful. We bought some of everything for everyone. Half of what we got we didn't need. We just had fun buying it. We got back to the hotel around 6:00 p.m., took a bath and sat around talking and watching TV. We ate while we were out so we weren't hungry. I was tired and so was Helen. We fell off to sleep holding each other. I woke up at 10:45 p.m. and boy was I in the mood. I started kissing her from head to toe. She awoke and started pulling at me begging me to give her every thing I had and I was willing to accommodate her. We rocked nonstop for twenty minutes. Our bodies were wet with perspiration. Neither one of us wanted it to end but we couldn't hold back any longer. We climaxed together. It was like I was trying to merge my body and soul with hers. This time neither one of us were able to move. We fell asleep right there, never making it to either bedroom.

A WELCOME HOME PARTY?

We didn't wake up until around noon on Sunday. I was so hungry I could have eaten a horse. We decided to get something to eat and get an early start getting back to the city. I pulled up to Kathy's place around 5:00 p.m. Kathy's car was gone. Annie would be at the shelter. She spent ninety percent of her time there helping people. I helped Helen get all her things out of the car. We kissed and kissed again. We were acting like school kids. I looked around and I saw a few curtains moving. I knew some of the neighbors were watching us. Helen said, "We better stop this."

"Oh no. Let's just give them something to talk about."

We stood there for a few more minutes and then we got everything inside to where it belonged. I said good night and drove home. No wonder Kathy wasn't home. She was at my house. Everyone except Rachel was at my house. It was almost like having a coming home party. Mom was the first one at the door.

"Mann, you're back. Where is Helen?"

"I took her home. I didn't know you were planning a welcome home party for us!!"

"We just decided that we would."

"How did you know what time we would get back?"

"We just took a chance. We have only been waiting for about a hour and a half. Kathy, Annie and Roger just got here."

Everybody was trying to talk at once.

"Wait, wait, please one at a time."

J.J. ran up to me and said, "Is the box empty?"

"Yes it is."

"All right!! Way to go Dad!!"

Everybody started slapping their hands together and saying congratulations to me.

"When is the big day?"

"Maybe we can have a double ceremony," said Kathy.

"You mean…."

"Yes, you and Helen and Roger and me."

We told everyone about the good news. By that time Helen walked into the room. Roger had called her and asked her to come over right away. She was running. I think she thought something was wrong. It only took a few minutes to realize that everything was okay. We filled her in on what we had been discussing before she arrived. We sat around later on eating and drinking. People came until about 10:00 p.m. And then everyone left. Liz and all three of the kids were in my room. Brandy wanted to know if she could be a flower girl. Randy wanted to be the ring barer. J.J. decided he wanted to be my best man. Liz said,

"You think Helen will allow me to be her maid of honor?"

"I don't see why not. You'll have to ask her though."

"Look you guys we can continue this some other time. I have to get some rest and you have school tomorrow. We all said good night and went to our perspective rooms.

The next day I went to work with a grin on my face that no *mortician* could wipe off. John stood there looking. I didn't give him a chance to say anything.

"Yes. Yes. Yes to whatever question you are going to ask."

"Well congratulations. I am very happy for the two of you. Any chance I could be best man?"

"J.J. already put his request in. But we need one for Roger."

"Well, I am available. Just let me know."

The week went by pretty fast. I had lunch with Helen every day that I could. That Friday, Rachel came by my office. I knew we were about to argue so I wanted to stop it before it got started. She said, "I heard you are planning on getting married again."

"Why should that come as a surprise to you? You are living with Charles. You have one child and another on the way."

"Who told you I was pregnant again?"

"You just did!!"

"Well, I hope she is good to my kids."

"She is very good to our children and they love her as much as I do."

It didn't take long for her to tone it down. It seemed as if she was different in a way.

"James, I know I have no right to ask, but was there anything between you and Helen after we were married?"

"No there wasn't as a matter-of-fact. There was never anyone but you the entire time until recently."

"You waited that long?"

"Yes, Rachel. I did."

"James, I am sorry, I am so sorry."

"Well we can't go back. We just have to move forward. I just hope we can be friends. We don't need to show hate and animosity around the kids."

"James, I don't hate you."

"I don't hate you either Rachel."

"James, I wish you all the luck in the world and happiness. I just want the kids to be happy. I realize now that it's not about me. It's about what is best for them."

"Rachel, I wouldn't get into a relationship that my children weren't happy with."

I didn't want to hurt her feelings because everyone knew no one in the family cared much about Charles. Randy and Brandy really disliked him. They wouldn't say anything in front of me but I have overheard them talking to J.J. In addition Liz told me a few things they had mentioned to her about him.

"James, I thank you for making a visitation arrangement that would allow me to see the children and be a part of their lives. If it had been the other way around, I know I would have been a total bitch just out of spite. I have learned so much about forgiveness from you and your family. I am not mad at my father anymore. I now know that he had nothing to do with my mother's death. I just needed someone to blame and that was easier than dealing with her death."

"Well, Rachel you know that I believe that "you reap what you sow." On that note, we will let the past stay dead and move forward from here. You know you are a part of the family and you always have the support of all of us. You have your father and now you will have Kathy as your stepmother. You two seem to get along okay."

"Yes we do. We had a long talk and now it looks like she is going to be my stepmother. We have gotten on much better terms than we were in the past. I love my father. I will try to get along with her for that reason."

This was a new Rachel. It was hard to believe that she was now behaving like a mature woman and not the selfish little girl I once knew. This was a mature woman that had her priorities in check.

"James thank you for letting me take up so much of your time. I'm going to run along now." When she got to the door, she hugged me and said, "Thank you again."

"Take care of yourself," I said and I really meant it.

IT CAN'T GET ANY BETTER THAN THIS

I was up bright and early looking like Chef Boy R D. That's the name Liz and J.J. gave me a few years ago. Liz was handling the salad and the cold items for the cook out. I was working on all the meats. I couldn't keep my mind off of Helen. Everyone arrived around 1:00 p.m. John was the last to arrive as usual. We had the music going and everyone was talking and being social to each other. Kathy was the first to speak. Her and Mom were standing side by side. I was flipping burgers as usual.

"Everyone knows that Roger and I are getting married."

Everyone started saying congratulations and was hugging them. Then the question came.

"When is the date?"

"Wait, wait. There is more. I think we might be having a double ceremony. There is one more couple in this family that you all know about right James and Helen?"

I couldn't say anything. Helen got choked up on a hot dog she was eating and all eyes were on us. We hadn't set a date yet. I stepped up but my purpose was not to embarrass us. Mom and Kathy were both smiling. I took a glimpse at Rachel's face. She had a genuine smile.

"Yes, people I've asked Helen to marry me as most of you know and she said yes. We haven't set a date but I am waiting and hoping. I don't want to rush her."

"How about the double ceremony? J.J. can be my best man and John can be yours," Roger said.

"What about the bride's maids?"

"Ida will be my bride's maid and Liz can be Helen's if it is okay with her."

"How about two weeks from today which is October 16?"

"That sounds good to me." I walked over and hugged Helen. She had made me the happiest man alive.

"Do you think you can be ready in two weeks baby?"

"Honey, I could be ready tomorrow."

Everyone started laughing.

"So it's set. We'll have a double ceremony on October sixteen."

For the next fourteen days that's all we talked about.

A DAY TO REMEMBER

Bobby, my brother, gave Helen away and Annie gave Kathy away. The wedding was so lovely that I had to stand back and take another look. I didn't see Helen's dress before the wedding because of the old tradition that the groom shouldn't see his bride until she enters the church. She wore a long white dress that sat off the shoulders. It resembled a ball gown with a V shape in the back and a tiara style headpiece, which held a long veil that turned into an extended lace train.

Kathy's dress was a sleeveless off white floor length dress with a short lace veil. All of the guys were decked out in black tuxedoes. I must say that we looked good. Some of the pictures from the wedding ended up in one of the local magazines and we looked good. Mom sent a lot of pictures to Jackson, Mississippi and to other family members. The reception was held in the church dining room area, which could seat 500 people easily. After the cutting of the cakes everything was done in fours, Kathy and Roger and Helen and me. It was a woman's dream to have a day like this. Mom was Kathy's bride's maid but Rachel was the matron of honor. Rachel caught one of the bouquets and Liz's girlfriend caught the other one. Liz didn't even reach for it. She just smiled at me. This was indeed a day to remember. Helen and I decided to go to New York up around Niagara Falls for our honeymoon. Kathy and Roger took off for the Virgin Islands. I chose Niagara Falls because of the water. I have a thing about water. I must say it was everything that I expected and more. I've always wanted to make love close to the falls. It's something about it that just fascinates me. I was a little worried about the honeymoon. I thought that there was nothing we could do that we hadn't done already but boy was I wrong. After we settled in, Helen went to change clothes. She came out of the bathroom with nothing but a red ribbon on that said, "I am yours for life." For 39, the girl looked good. I mean really good.

She walked over to me and took my hand. She slowly led me toward the bed. After she lay back on the bed and turned on a small radio, she seductively asked me to strip very slowly. The sounds of Freddie Jackson could be heard from the radio. I did as I was told as the melodies of Freddie Jackson flowed through my head. It took all of 10 minutes after the socks. I stood very still knowing what was going to happen and feeling as though I'd been waiting forever. Then there was a switch. Helen pulled me face down and sat across my buttocks. I could feel the warmness between her thighs and the warm liquid on my skin. I had never had a hot oil treatment before. Her touch was so sensual and her fingers felt like little feathers. Then there was a real feather. I almost jumped off the bed. Never in my life had I felt this kind of gentleness before. I've made good love before but never have I experienced foreplay like this before. No sooner then I got control of myself, she coached me into turning over on my back during which time (as I was told) the pleasure was repeated just as slow and with as much care. It was clear that Helen was in the driver's seat. This time I was just along for the ride. Lying there with my eyes closed, I was thinking that I must think of something really great for our first anniversary. As the oil trailed down my body, Helen would blow her warm breath making the oil feel even warmer. Then there was the feather again. First around my ear and then on each nipple, my belly button, my groin area and even my toes. I was beside myself with pleasure. I was so ready until I thought I was going to explode. Just as I couldn't take any more, Helen started kissing my eyes, nose, and mouth with real passionate kisses just like ten years ago. Then she bought her hot love cave down on my man hood, which was standing at attention all while making sure not to hurt her. Helen always had trouble taking all of me even lying on her back. With gentleness we both were in ecstasy. She felt so good that all I could do was to keep from pulling her trying to get deeper and deeper. I held my cool. I could feel the torture. She was there and I could let go also. I could feel the warm liquid running all around our genital area. The woman never ceased to amaze me. In everything she did, I was there also.

I can say that our honeymoon was a new experience. Helen had a lot of tricks in her bag and she assured me that it was only the beginning and it sure was.

..........SIX YEARS LATER............

I guess things can be so good that you have to stop and ask yourself why. Everything seems to be going well. Helen and I have been married for six years. During that time I have assisted in opening 14 dialysis units nationwide. J.J. was currently doing his internship/residency to become a doctor. Randy and Brandy were both in high school. Rachel was back on the playing field after Charles death. We all knew he had some mysterious disease but she never really talked about it. Her kids were always at our house and they would talk. Randy and Brandy would pick up on things and convey a message.

They say that in each life some rain must fall. I got up with the feeling that something was wrong or going to go wrong. I saw the kids off to school.

Helen had some shopping to do so I got into the office late. I took a detour to get a much-needed cup of coffee. In the cafeteria, I really wasn't listening but I heard someone say 'that's the school Mr. Bradshaw's kids go to. Then I looked up and saw the news flash on the television:

SHOOTING AT LANSFIELD.

"There were three children shot, one seriously injured…"

By the time I heard the voice on the intercom, "Paging Mr. Bradshaw. Report to your office please," I was running to my office. When I got there the school was on the phone. The conversation and the drive to the school are events that seem to have passed without actually happening. I looked up and I was running into the principal's office. I hadn't made it to the office when a voice stopped me.

"Mr. Bradshaw." It was Randy's homeroom teacher, Mrs. Lee. "I am so sorry. They took Randy to the hospital. I am sure that he will be fine! Would you mind if I came along with you? My teaching assistant will watch my class. I want to make sure he's okay. I want to see for myself."

By the time I got to St. James Hospital, Rachel was there already. I had to calm her down because she was a little hysterical. I thought Randy was dead. I wanted to know how my son was doing. Before I could ask the charge nurse, a doctor was present to answer my questions.

"Mr. Bradshaw I am Dr. Sam Young. I recognize you from your picture last year in our dialysis workshop. I am caring for Randy. He is fine with the exception of being a little shaken up. Come with me."

I took a breath of relief.

"Thank God, thank God."

"The bullet hit him in his left arm just above the elbow. It will be a little sore but he is just fine and has been asking for you."

Randy jumped up the minute he saw me.

"Dad." He was trying hard to fight back the tears. Mrs. Lee spoke. I was so concerned about my son that I forgot she was present in the room.

"I am sorry. Dr. Young this is Mrs. Lee, Randy's teacher. She wanted to see for herself that Randy was going to be okay."

Randy was still holding on to me. Rachel walked in. She was under control. They treated Randy for a minor gun shot wound and released him. We were on our way home when I realized that I hadn't paged Helen. She was in an uproar. Mom, Kathy, Liz, Roger among other family members were going crazy with worry. Just when I thought things had gotten back to normal, two weeks later I found out that Brandy was experimenting with speed. J.J. picked up on it and brought it to my attention. For the first time in my life, I didn't know how to handle a situation. I didn't want to lose my daughter to drugs. For the first time in a long time I cried like a baby. I didn't want Helen to see me so broken down and defeated. I didn't want to appear as if I was falling apart but I knew I needed help. I needed some spiritual guidance. I picked up a Bible for the first time in years. It fell open on Isaiah 54:17. "No weapon that is formed against thee shall prosper." I knew then what I had to do. I went to Brandy's room. I knocked.

"Come in."

"Brandy we have to talk."

"J.J. talked to you didn't he?"

"Yes, he did. He did the right thing too. I'm glad it's out."

"Dad, I am not hooked, I only tried a little cocaine and speed. It wasn't something that I could fall in love with. I doubt if I will ever try it again. I stopped hanging around the kids that were doing it. They didn't have dreams nor did they think about a future Dad. I'm no fool." I couldn't believe she was saying all of this but somehow I believed her. "Dad please don't tell Mom, Grandma, Ida, or Kathy. I will do anything if you don't tell them. I never did anything harsh to support what I was doing like stealing and it only went on for a month. I've gotten myself together. I was able to think and make the right decision."

"Okay, we have a treatment program at the hospital. I won't say anything if you get into it." She agreed. She cooperated and I didn't tell anyone.

It's been two years now and looking back there has been blood, sweat, and tears but God brought us through it all. Our strength is that we stay connected. With love, understanding, and patience, families can withstand the tests of time. It turned out that Mom and Kathy already knew about Brandy long before I did. They just didn't know what kind of drug it was or how long she had been using. They said that some things are best dealt with through the parent and I'm glad. It would have destroyed her if she knew that they knew.

Brandy decided not to go away to college like J.J. and Randy. She wanted to stay close to home. I was glad. She is at a local city college and doing fine. She is working with other young people that had the same problem that she had years ago. Her motto is with a good family you can come back from any thing. J.J. is a doctor on staff at the hospital doing his residency. Randy is in the NASA program. He is close to realizing his dream of becoming an astronaut and I know he will make it.

We just found out last year what Charles died from. It was AIDS. Rachel recently tested positive for the HIV Virus but she is doing fine thanks to medical technology. Helen and I have been tested twice and thank God we have tested negative. I was afraid of what those tests would reveal because I was still married to Rachel when she started sleeping with Charles. We don't know how long he was infected but she has the support of the family behind her. Roger and Kathy are happy beyond any one dream. Mom and Liz are off to the Holy Land. Liz won 3.5 million dollars in the Florida State lottery. They are gone all the time, which was a dream of Liz's all along, to travel.

Everyone is married, working or in school but we always get together once a month for the weekend. Helen and I always communicate with each other, which is what makes a good marriage stay together. As a family, we believe the key to weathering all storms is to stay connected.

Ida W. Byther-Smith was born in Terry, Mississippi, is the oldest of ten children, and is the mother of four children. At age 41, she tested positive for HIV, and her life completely changed. After almost dying she now says, "I thank God for HIV." I did not learn to live until I almost died."

She has done numerous TV interviews and has also written or appeared in articles in Ebony Magazine, POZ Magazine, The Tribune, Sun Times, and Chicago Defender. She speaks as an advocate for those living with HIV with the compassion that only comes through personal experience.

At least once a week, she is somewhere trying to help people to understand that "even though it may not be your fault you are positive, it is your responsibility to get tested and know." She works especially with church groups and people over 50 to get the message of valuing yourself and walking in courage for those who often feel misused and ashamed.

One of her major goals is to disseminate information to women about the HIV/Aids epidemic since women face special risks and are dying faster because of their lack of knowledge.

She gives groups educational presentations on prevention and care of HIV/Aids. She is a living testimony of what God can do. Ms. Byther-Smith is a graduate of Malcolm X College receiving an AAS in 1985. She went on to Governor State University where she received her BA in 1988. She is currently working on a Master's Degree in Theology.